A Love Worth Waiting For

Christian romance fiction, Volume 1

Angela Marie Stewart

Published by B&H Publishing Group, 2024.

This is a work of fiction. Similarities to real people, places, or events are entirely coincidental.

A LOVE WORTH WAITING FOR

First edition. August 21, 2024.

Copyright © 2024 Angela Marie Stewart.

ISBN: 979-8227884749

Written by Angela Marie Stewart.

Table of Contents

To those who have waited with faith, prayed with hope, and loved
with patience—this book is for you.

May you find comfort in knowing that your journey is not in vain, and
that the love worth waiting for is always held in the hands of a faithful
God.

And to my Savior, who is the ultimate fulfillment of every desire,
thank You for teaching me the true meaning of love.

Chapter 1: The Virtue of Patience

Theological Reflection: Explore the biblical concept of patience as a virtue, particularly in the context of waiting for true love. Reference James 5:7-8 and discuss how patience in love is a reflection of faith in God's timing.

Introduction: The Beauty of Waiting

IN AN AGE OF INSTANT gratification, the virtue of patience is often overlooked, undervalued, and misunderstood. The modern world encourages us to seek immediate results, whether in our careers, personal ambitions, or relationships. The idea of waiting—especially for something as profound and life-altering as love—can seem archaic, unnecessary, or even a sign of weakness. Yet, patience is deeply rooted in the Christian faith and is a critical element in our spiritual journey, particularly when it comes to matters of the heart.

The Bible presents patience as a fundamental virtue, a reflection of trust in God's plan, and a crucial component of our relationships with others. It is especially significant in the context of waiting for true love, where patience is not just about enduring time but is a testament to one's faith, hope, and commitment to God's timing.

In James 5:7-8, we find a powerful exhortation to embrace patience: *"Be patient, therefore, brothers, until the coming of the Lord. See how the farmer waits for the precious fruit of the earth, being patient about it, until it receives the early and the late rains. You also, be patient. Establish your hearts, for the coming of the Lord is at hand."* This passage not only encourages patience but likens it to the farmer's careful and hopeful waiting for the fruits of his labor, trusting in the natural process and in God's provision.

This chapter delves into the virtue of patience as it relates to love, exploring how this quality shapes our relationships, aligns our hearts with God's will, and ultimately leads us to a love worth waiting for.

The Biblical Foundation of Patience

TO UNDERSTAND THE IMPORTANCE of patience in the context of love, we must first grasp its biblical foundation. The Bible is replete with teachings on patience, which is often closely linked with faith, perseverance, and hope.

One of the most well-known verses on patience is found in Galatians 5:22-23, where patience is listed as one of the fruits of the Spirit: *"But the fruit of the Spirit is love, joy, peace, patience, kindness, goodness, faithfulness, gentleness, self-control; against such things there is no law."* Here, patience is presented not merely as an optional virtue but as a natural outcome of a life led by the Spirit.

In the Old Testament, patience is often associated with the idea of waiting on the Lord. Psalm 27:14 instructs, *"Wait for the Lord; be strong, and let your heart take courage; wait for the Lord!"* This verse encapsulates the essence of biblical patience: a strong, courageous, and hopeful waiting that is grounded in trust in God's timing.

The story of Abraham is a quintessential example of patience in the Bible. God promised Abraham that he would be the father of many nations, yet he and his wife Sarah had to wait many years for the fulfillment of this promise. Their journey was marked by moments of doubt and impatience, as seen in their decision to take matters into their own hands with Hagar, which led to the birth of Ishmael. However, the eventual birth of Isaac, the child of promise, is a powerful reminder that God's timing is perfect and that patience is often rewarded with blessings far beyond our expectations.

The New Testament continues this theme, emphasizing the importance of patience in the life of a believer. Romans 12:12 exhorts Christians to be *"rejoicing in hope, patient in tribulation, constant in prayer."* Patience is not just about waiting passively; it involves active endurance, perseverance, and a steadfast commitment to God's promises.

Patience in the Context of Love

PATIENCE IS PARTICULARLY significant when it comes to love, as true love often requires us to wait—sometimes for a long time, sometimes in ways that test our faith and resolve. The world often portrays love as a whirlwind of emotions, an instant connection, or a spontaneous spark. However, the Bible presents a different picture of love, one that is patient, deliberate, and deeply rooted in commitment and sacrifice.

In 1 Corinthians 13:4, we read, *"Love is patient, love is kind. It does not envy, it does not boast, it is not proud."* This verse is often quoted in wedding ceremonies, but its implications go far beyond the marital vows. It teaches us that love, in its truest form, is patient. It is willing to wait, to endure, and to trust in the timing and the process.

But what does it mean to be patient in love? It means waiting for the right person, the right time, and the right circumstances, all according to God's plan. It means resisting the urge to rush into relationships out of loneliness or fear, and instead, allowing love to grow naturally and healthily. It means trusting that God knows what is best for us and that He will bring the right person into our lives at the right time.

This kind of patience is not passive. It requires active faith, perseverance, and a deep trust in God's goodness and timing. It means being willing to wait for God's best, even when the waiting is difficult or when we are tempted to settle for less than what God has planned for us.

Patience as a Reflection of Faith

AT ITS CORE, PATIENCE in love is a reflection of faith. When we wait patiently for love, we are expressing our trust in God's sovereignty and His perfect timing. We are acknowledging that He knows what is best for us, and we are willing to wait for His plan to unfold in our lives.

This kind of faith is not always easy. It requires us to let go of our own desires, our own timelines, and our own control. It requires us to surrender to God's will, even when we don't understand it or when it seems to be taking longer than we expected.

But this surrender is not a sign of weakness; it is a sign of strength. It takes great courage to wait patiently for love, to trust that God is at work even when we cannot see it, and to believe that He will bring the right person into our lives at the right time.

In James 5:7-8, we are encouraged to be patient like the farmer who waits for the precious fruit of the earth. The farmer does not see the fruit immediately; he must wait for the early and late rains. But he waits with hope and expectation, trusting that the harvest will come in due time.

In the same way, we are called to wait patiently for love, trusting that God is at work even when we cannot see it. We are called to wait with hope and expectation, believing that God's timing is perfect and that He will bring the right person into our lives at the right time.

The Challenges of Patience in Love

WAITING FOR LOVE IS not always easy. In fact, it can be one of the most challenging aspects of our spiritual journey. The world around us often tells us that we should not have to wait for anything, that we deserve instant gratification, and that we should take matters into our own hands if things are not happening quickly enough.

This mindset can lead to impatience, frustration, and even despair, especially when it comes to love. We may begin to question God's timing, wondering why He is taking so long to bring the right person into our lives. We may be tempted to settle for less than God's best, thinking that any relationship is better than being alone. We may even begin to doubt God's goodness, wondering if He really has a good plan for our love lives.

These challenges are real, and they can be difficult to overcome. But they are also opportunities for us to grow in our faith and our trust in God. When we face the challenges of waiting for love, we have the chance to deepen our relationship with God, to strengthen our faith, and to learn to rely on Him more fully.

One of the key challenges of patience in love is the temptation to settle for less than God's best. When we are tired of waiting, we may be tempted to enter into a relationship that is not healthy or that does not align with God's will for our lives. We may be tempted to lower our standards, to compromise our values, or to accept someone who is not God's best for us simply because we are tired of waiting.

But settling for less than God's best is never the answer. It may bring temporary relief from loneliness or impatience, but it will ultimately lead to heartache and disappointment. God's plans for us are always good, and His timing is always perfect. When we wait patiently for His best, we can trust that He will bring the right person into our lives at the right time.

Another challenge of patience in love is the struggle with loneliness. Waiting for love can be a lonely journey, especially when it seems like everyone around us is in a relationship. We may feel left out, overlooked, or forgotten, and these feelings can be difficult to bear.

But loneliness is not a sign that something is wrong with us or that God has forgotten us. It is a natural part of the waiting process, and it can be an opportunity for us to draw closer to God. When we feel lonely, we can turn to God for comfort, knowing that He is always with us and that He understands our pain.

Psalm 23:4 reminds us that even when we walk through the darkest valleys, God is with us. He is our Shepherd, our Comforter, and our Guide, and He will never leave us or forsake us. When we feel lonely in our waiting, we can find solace in His presence and trust that He is at work, even in the silence.

The Rewards of Patience in Love

WHILE THE CHALLENGES of waiting for love are real, the rewards are even greater. When we wait patiently for love, we position ourselves to receive God's best for our lives. We allow Him to work in our hearts, to prepare us for the relationship He has for us, and to bring the right person into our lives at the right time.

One of the greatest rewards of patience in love is the peace that comes from knowing we are in God's will. When we wait patiently for His timing, we can rest in the assurance that He is in control and that He knows what is best for us. We can let go of our anxiety, our fear, and our need to control, and we can trust that God is working all things together for our good.

Another reward of patience in love is the joy that comes from receiving God's best. When we wait for His timing, we can trust that the person He brings into our lives will be the one who complements us, supports us, and helps us grow in our faith. We can trust that our relationship will be built on a strong foundation of mutual love, respect, and commitment, and that it will be a source of joy, fulfillment, and blessing.

But perhaps the greatest reward of patience in love is the deeper relationship with God that comes from waiting. When we wait patiently for His timing, we learn to rely on Him more fully, to trust Him more deeply, and to love Him more passionately. We learn to find our identity, our worth, and our fulfillment in Him alone, and we discover that He is the true source of all love.

In Isaiah 40:31, we are reminded that *"those who wait for the Lord shall renew their strength; they shall mount up with wings like eagles; they shall run and not be weary; they shall walk and not faint."* When we wait patiently for love, we are renewed, strengthened, and empowered by God's grace. We are lifted up by His love, and we are equipped to love others with the same patience, kindness, and grace that He has shown us.

Practical Steps to Cultivate Patience in Love

CULTIVATING PATIENCE in love is a journey, and it requires intentionality, prayer, and a deep reliance on God's grace. Here are some practical steps to help you grow in patience as you wait for love:

1. Pray for Patience: Begin by asking God to cultivate the fruit of patience in your heart. Prayer is a powerful tool, and when you ask God to help you wait patiently for love, He will give you the strength and grace you need.

2. Trust in God's Timing: Remind yourself regularly that God's timing is perfect, and that He knows what is best for you. Trust that He is at work in your life, even when you cannot see it, and that He will bring the right person into your life at the right time.

3. Focus on Your Relationship with God: Use this time of waiting to draw closer to God. Spend time in prayer, reading the Bible, and worshiping Him. The more you focus on your relationship with God, the more you will find peace, contentment, and fulfillment in Him alone.

4. Guard Your Heart: Be intentional about guarding your heart during this time of waiting. Avoid situations or relationships that could lead you to compromise your values or settle for less than God's best. Instead, focus on becoming the person God has called you to be, and trust that He will bring the right person into your life when the time is right.

5. Surround Yourself with Supportive Community: Seek out a community of believers who can support you in your journey of waiting for love. Surround yourself with friends, family, and mentors who will encourage you, pray for you, and help you stay focused on God's plan for your life.

6. Embrace Contentment in Singleness: Learn to find contentment and joy in your current season of singleness. Instead of focusing on what you lack, focus on the opportunities you have to grow, serve, and make a difference in the lives of others.

7. Practice Gratitude: Cultivate an attitude of gratitude by regularly thanking God for the blessings in your life. Gratitude will help you stay positive, focused, and hopeful as you wait for love.

8. Be Patient with Yourself: Remember that patience is a journey, and it is okay to struggle at times. Be kind to yourself, and give yourself grace as you

navigate the challenges of waiting for love. Trust that God is working in your life, even in the moments of doubt, frustration, or loneliness.

Conclusion: A Love Worth Waiting For

PATIENCE IN LOVE IS not just about enduring time; it is about trusting in God's perfect timing and His good plans for our lives. It is about waiting with hope, faith, and expectation, knowing that God is at work even when we cannot see it. It is about surrendering our desires, our timelines, and our control to God, and trusting that He knows what is best for us.

As we wait patiently for love, we have the opportunity to grow in our relationship with God, to deepen our faith, and to become the person He has called us to be. We have the chance to build a strong foundation for our future relationships, one that is rooted in patience, trust, and commitment to God's will.

And when the time is right, we can trust that God will bring the right person into our lives, someone who will complement us, support us, and help us grow in our faith. We can trust that our love will be one that is worth waiting for, one that is built on a strong foundation of mutual love, respect, and commitment to God's plan.

So, as you wait for love, remember the words of James 5:7-8: *"Be patient, therefore, brothers, until the coming of the Lord. See how the farmer waits for the precious fruit of the earth, being patient about it, until it receives the early and the late rains. You also, be patient. Establish your hearts, for the coming of the Lord is at hand."* Let these words encourage you, strengthen you, and guide you as you wait for the love that God has in store for you—a love that is truly worth waiting for.

Chapter 2: Faith in God's Plan

Theological Reflection: Reflect on trusting God's plan for one's life, especially in matters of the heart. Incorporate Jeremiah 29:11, emphasizing that God's plans are for our good, including in relationships.

Introduction: The Divine Blueprint

IN THE COMPLEX TAPESTRY of life, one of the most challenging yet profoundly important lessons for a believer is learning to trust in God's plan. This is especially true in matters of the heart, where emotions run deep, desires can cloud judgment, and the future often seems uncertain. Trusting in God's plan requires faith, surrender, and a deep belief that God's intentions for us are always rooted in love and goodness.

Jeremiah 29:11 is one of the most cherished verses in the Bible, offering reassurance and hope: *"For I know the plans I have for you, declares the Lord, plans for welfare and not for evil, to give you a future and a hope."* This verse encapsulates the essence of God's relationship with us—His children. It is a reminder that God is not only aware of our circumstances but has also meticulously designed a plan for our lives that leads to our ultimate good.

But how does this divine blueprint play out in the realm of relationships? How do we navigate the complexities of love, dating, marriage, and even heartbreak while holding onto the belief that God's plan is unfolding perfectly? This chapter delves into the importance of trusting God's plan in our romantic lives, exploring how faith can guide us through the uncertainties and lead us to the love that He has prepared for us.

Understanding God's Sovereignty

TO FULLY TRUST IN GOD'S plan, especially in matters as personal as our relationships, we must first understand the concept of God's sovereignty. God's sovereignty means that He is the supreme authority over all things—nothing happens outside of His will or control. This includes every aspect of our lives, from the seemingly mundane to the most significant, including our relationships.

The Bible is clear about God's sovereignty over our lives. Proverbs 16:9 says, *"The heart of man plans his way, but the Lord establishes his steps."* This verse highlights the tension between our human desire to plan and control our lives and the reality that it is God who ultimately directs our paths. While we may have hopes, dreams, and plans for our relationships, it is God who knows the bigger picture and is guiding us toward His intended outcome.

When it comes to relationships, understanding God's sovereignty means recognizing that He knows what is best for us, even when we do not. It means trusting that He is in control, even when our plans do not unfold as we expected. This trust is not always easy, especially when we face disappointment, heartbreak, or prolonged seasons of waiting. However, it is in these moments of uncertainty that our faith in God's sovereignty is tested and strengthened.

The Human Desire for Control

ONE OF THE GREATEST challenges to trusting in God's plan is our innate desire for control. As human beings, we crave certainty and security, and we often try to achieve these through our own efforts. This desire for control can be especially strong in our romantic lives, where we may feel vulnerable or uncertain about the future.

In relationships, the desire for control can manifest in various ways. We might try to force a relationship to work, even when it is clear that it is not God's will. We might rush into a relationship out of fear of being alone, rather than waiting for God's timing. Or we might become anxious and frustrated when our plans do not unfold as we had hoped, questioning God's goodness and faithfulness.

However, the desire for control is ultimately an illusion. No matter how much we try to control our lives and relationships, we are not in charge—God is. He is the one who knows the beginning from the end, and He is the one who is guiding our lives according to His perfect plan.

Letting go of our desire for control and surrendering to God's plan requires a shift in perspective. It means acknowledging that we do not have all the answers and that we cannot see the full picture. It means trusting that God is working all things together for our good, even when we do not understand how.

JEREMIAH 29:11: A PROMISE of Hope

Jeremiah 29:11 is often quoted as a source of comfort and encouragement, especially during times of uncertainty. The verse is part of a letter that the prophet Jeremiah wrote to the Israelites who were living in exile in Babylon. The Israelites were in a difficult and uncertain situation—they had been taken from their homeland, and their future seemed bleak. Yet, in the midst of their exile, God spoke words of hope and reassurance through Jeremiah.

"For I know the plans I have for you, declares the Lord, plans for welfare and not for evil, to give you a future and a hope."

This promise was not just for the Israelites; it is a promise for all of God's children. It is a reminder that, no matter what circumstances we find ourselves in, God has a plan for our lives—a plan that is good, hopeful, and full of purpose.

In the context of relationships, Jeremiah 29:11 offers a powerful reminder that God is intimately involved in our romantic lives. He knows our desires, our fears, and our hopes, and He has a plan for our love lives that is for our ultimate good. This plan may not always align with our own desires or timelines, but it is a plan that is rooted in God's love for us.

Trusting in this promise means believing that God is working behind the scenes, orchestrating the details of our lives in ways that we cannot see or understand. It means trusting that, even when we face disappointment or heartache, God is still in control and that His plan is still unfolding perfectly.

God's Plan in the Midst of Waiting

ONE OF THE MOST CHALLENGING aspects of trusting in God's plan is the experience of waiting. Waiting can be difficult, especially in a culture that values instant gratification. In matters of the heart, waiting can feel especially painful—whether it is waiting for the right person to come into our lives, waiting for a relationship to move forward, or waiting for healing after a breakup.

However, the Bible is clear that waiting is an essential part of the Christian life. Throughout Scripture, we see examples of God's people waiting on Him—Abraham and Sarah waiting for the promised child, Joseph waiting for his dreams to be fulfilled, and the Israelites waiting for deliverance from Egypt. In each of these stories, we see that waiting is not wasted time; it is a period of preparation, growth, and dependence on God.

In the context of relationships, waiting is an opportunity to grow in our faith and trust in God. It is a time to deepen our relationship with Him, to develop patience and perseverance, and to become the person He has called us to be. Waiting allows us to align our hearts with God's will, to surrender our desires to Him, and to trust that He is working all things together for our good.

Psalm 27:14 encourages us to *"Wait for the Lord; be strong, and let your heart take courage; wait for the Lord!"* This verse reminds us that waiting is not passive; it requires strength, courage, and a steadfast trust in God. It is a time to be patient, to trust in God's timing, and to believe that He will fulfill His promises to us.

The Role of Prayer in Trusting God's Plan

PRAYER IS A VITAL COMPONENT of trusting in God's plan, especially in matters of the heart. Through prayer, we communicate with God, share our desires and concerns, and seek His guidance and wisdom. Prayer is also a way of surrendering our plans to God and asking Him to align our hearts with His will.

In Philippians 4:6-7, Paul encourages us to bring our requests to God in prayer: *"Do not be anxious about anything, but in everything by prayer and supplication with thanksgiving let your requests be made known to God. And the peace of God, which surpasses all understanding, will guard your hearts and your minds in Christ Jesus."*

When we pray about our relationships, we are acknowledging that we need God's help and guidance. We are inviting Him into the process and asking Him to lead us according to His plan. Prayer also helps us to release our anxiety and fear, as we place our trust in God and His perfect timing.

In the context of relationships, prayer can take many forms. It might involve praying for wisdom and discernment in making decisions, praying for patience and perseverance during times of waiting, or praying for healing and restoration after a breakup. Whatever the situation, prayer is a powerful tool for deepening our trust in God and aligning our hearts with His plan.

Surrendering to God's Plan

SURRENDER IS A KEY aspect of trusting in God's plan. Surrender means letting go of our own desires, plans, and control, and placing our lives in God's hands. It is an act of faith, a recognition that God's ways are higher than our ways, and that His plans are always for our good.

In Proverbs 3:5-6, we are instructed to *"Trust in the Lord with all your heart, and do not lean on your own understanding. In all your ways acknowledge him, and he will make straight your paths."* This verse highlights the importance of surrendering our own understanding and trusting in God's guidance.

In relationships, surrender might mean letting go of a relationship that is not aligned with God's will, even if it is painful. It might mean trusting God's timing, even when it feels like He is taking too long. Or it might mean releasing our own desires and plans, and asking God to lead us according to His will.

Surrender is not easy—it requires humility, faith, and a willingness to let go of our own control. However, it is through surrender that we experience the peace and joy that come from trusting in God's plan. When we surrender our relationships to God, we can rest in the assurance that He is in control, and that He is leading us toward His best for our lives.

Recognizing God's Hand in Our Relationships

AS WE TRUST IN GOD'S plan, it is important to recognize His hand at work in our relationships. God is not distant or uninvolved in our lives—He is actively guiding, directing, and orchestrating the details of our relationships.

One way to recognize God's hand in our relationships is by seeking His guidance and wisdom through prayer and Scripture. As we spend time in God's Word and in prayer, we can discern His will and direction for our lives. We can also seek the counsel of godly friends, family members, and mentors who can provide wisdom and insight.

Another way to recognize God's hand in our relationships is by looking for the fruit of the Spirit. Galatians 5:22-23 lists the fruit of the Spirit as *"love, joy, peace, patience, kindness, goodness, faithfulness, gentleness, self-control."* When we see these qualities evident in our relationships, it is a sign that God is at work, shaping and guiding us according to His plan.

Finally, we can recognize God's hand in our relationships by paying attention to His providence. God often guides us through the circumstances of our lives, opening doors that align with His will and closing doors that are not part of His plan. As we trust in His sovereignty, we can be confident that He is leading us toward His best for our lives.

Overcoming Doubts and Fears

TRUSTING IN GOD'S PLAN does not mean that we will never experience doubts or fears. In fact, doubts and fears are a natural part of the human experience, especially in matters as personal and significant as relationships. However, as believers, we are called to bring our doubts and fears to God, trusting that He is greater than our uncertainties.

One of the most powerful examples of overcoming doubt and fear in the Bible is the story of Jesus calming the storm. In Mark 4:35-41, we read about how Jesus and His disciples were caught in a fierce storm while crossing the Sea of Galilee. The disciples were terrified, fearing for their lives, but Jesus remained calm and rebuked the wind and the waves, saying, *"Peace! Be still!"* The storm ceased, and the disciples were filled with awe.

This story is a reminder that, no matter how fierce the storms of life may be, Jesus is in control. He is with us in the midst of our fears and doubts, and He has the power to bring peace to our hearts. When we are faced with doubts or fears about our relationships, we can turn to Jesus, asking Him to calm the storms in our hearts and to strengthen our faith.

Psalm 34:4 encourages us to seek God in our times of fear: *"I sought the Lord, and he answered me and delivered me from all my fears."* As we seek God in prayer, we can find comfort, peace, and reassurance, knowing that He is in control and that His plan for our lives is good.

The Role of Community in Trusting God's Plan

COMMUNITY PLAYS A VITAL role in helping us trust in God's plan for our relationships. As believers, we are not meant to navigate life's challenges alone—we are called to be part of a community of faith, where we can find support, encouragement, and accountability.

In Hebrews 10:24-25, we are instructed to *"consider how to stir up one another to love and good works, not neglecting to meet together, as is the habit of some, but encouraging one another, and all the more as you see the Day drawing near."* This verse emphasizes the importance of gathering together as believers, encouraging one another in our faith, and spurring one another on to love and good works.

In the context of relationships, community can provide valuable wisdom, guidance, and support. Whether it is through a small group, a mentorship relationship, or close friendships, being part of a community allows us to share our struggles, receive godly counsel, and be held accountable in our walk with Christ.

Community also helps us to stay focused on God's plan, especially when we are tempted to stray or to take matters into our own hands. When we are surrounded by fellow believers who are committed to following God's will, we are more likely to stay on the path that God has set before us.

Living Out Faith in God's Plan

TRUSTING IN GOD'S PLAN for our relationships is not a one-time decision; it is a daily commitment to live out our faith in practical ways. It involves aligning our actions, decisions, and attitudes with the belief that God's plan is good and that He is in control.

Living out faith in God's plan might involve making difficult decisions, such as ending a relationship that is not aligned with God's will, even when it is painful. It might involve waiting patiently for God's timing, even when we are tempted to rush ahead. Or it might involve choosing to love and forgive, even when it is challenging, trusting that God is at work in our hearts and in our relationships.

Colossians 3:17 reminds us to *"do everything in the name of the Lord Jesus, giving thanks to God the Father through him."* This verse encourages us to live our lives in a way that honors God, trusting that He is guiding our steps and that His plan for our lives is good.

As we live out our faith in God's plan, we can experience the peace and joy that come from knowing that we are in His will. We can rest in the assurance that God is leading us, and that He is working all things together for our good.

Conclusion: A Future and a Hope

JEREMIAH 29:11 OFFERS us a powerful promise of hope and a future. This promise is not just for the Israelites living in exile; it is for all of God's children who trust in His plan and surrender their lives to His will.

As we navigate the complexities of relationships, we can hold onto this promise, believing that God has a good plan for our love lives. We can trust that His timing is perfect, that His ways are higher than our ways, and that He is working all things together for our good.

Trusting in God's plan requires faith, surrender, and a deep belief that God's intentions for us are always rooted in love and goodness. It involves letting go of our own desires and control, and placing our lives in God's hands. It means waiting patiently for His timing, praying for His guidance, and seeking His will in every aspect of our lives.

As we trust in God's plan, we can experience the peace and joy that come from knowing that we are in His will. We can rest in the assurance that God is leading us, and that He is working all things together for our good. And we can look forward to the future with hope, knowing that God's plans for us are for our welfare, to give us a future and a hope—a love that is truly worth waiting for.

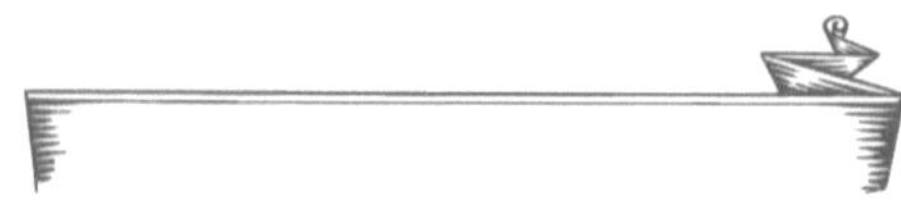

Chapter 3: Purity of Heart

Theological Reflection: Delve into the importance of maintaining purity while waiting for love. Discuss Matthew 5:8, where Jesus blesses the pure in heart, connecting it to the idea of waiting with a clean and sincere heart.

Introduction: The Call to Purity

IN THE SERMON ON THE Mount, Jesus presents a radical vision of the kingdom of God, one that upends the values and priorities of the world. Among His many teachings, the Beatitudes stand out as a series of blessings that define the character of those who belong to His kingdom. Matthew 5:8 declares, *"Blessed are the pure in heart, for they shall see God."* This statement is profound in its simplicity and yet deeply challenging in its implications. What does it mean to be pure in heart, and how does this purity relate to our relationships, especially in the context of waiting for love?

Purity of heart is not merely a matter of outward behavior; it is a condition of the inner life, a reflection of our deepest motivations, desires, and intentions. It involves a wholehearted devotion to God, a commitment to living in alignment with His will, and a sincere desire to honor Him in all areas of life—including our romantic relationships.

In a world that often equates love with passion, physical attraction, and immediate gratification, the call to purity may seem out of step with modern culture. Yet, for those who seek to follow Christ, maintaining purity of heart is essential not only for our spiritual well-being but also for building relationships that are rooted in love, trust, and respect.

This chapter explores the importance of maintaining purity while waiting for love, drawing from the teachings of Jesus in Matthew 5:8. We will delve into the biblical understanding of purity, the challenges we face in pursuing it, and the blessings that come from waiting with a clean and sincere heart.

The Biblical Concept of Purity

TO FULLY APPRECIATE the significance of purity of heart, it is important to understand the biblical concept of purity. In Scripture, purity is often associated with cleanliness, holiness, and separation from sin. It encompasses both moral and spiritual dimensions, reflecting a life that is free from corruption and dedicated to God.

In the Old Testament, the concept of purity is closely linked with the rituals and laws given to the Israelites. For example, the book of Leviticus contains numerous instructions on ceremonial cleanliness, emphasizing the importance of being pure before approaching God. These laws served as a reminder of God's holiness and the need for His people to be set apart from the surrounding nations.

However, the Old Testament also points to the deeper, inner aspect of purity. In Psalm 51:10, King David prays, *"Create in me a clean heart, O God, and renew a right spirit within me."* David recognizes that true purity goes beyond outward rituals; it is a matter of the heart. Similarly, the prophet Jeremiah speaks of the heart as the seat of human intentions, both good and evil: *"The heart is deceitful above all things, and desperately sick; who can understand it?"* (Jeremiah 17:9). This highlights the need for divine intervention to cleanse and purify the human heart.

In the New Testament, Jesus expands on this understanding of purity. In Matthew 15:18-20, He teaches that it is not what goes into a person's mouth that defiles them, but what comes out of the heart: *"But what comes out of the mouth proceeds from the heart, and this defiles a person. For out of the heart come evil thoughts, murder, adultery, sexual immorality, theft, false witness, slander. These are what defile a person."* Jesus shifts the focus from external observance to the internal condition of the heart, emphasizing that true purity is a matter of the inner life.

Matthew 5:8, where Jesus blesses the pure in heart, encapsulates this teaching. The pure in heart are those whose inner lives are aligned with God's will, whose thoughts, desires, and intentions are directed toward Him. They are not merely outwardly righteous but inwardly transformed by God's grace.

Purity in the Context of Waiting for Love

IN THE CONTEXT OF ROMANTIC relationships, maintaining purity of heart takes on special significance. Waiting for love with a pure heart means guarding our hearts, minds, and bodies from influences that can lead us away from God's will. It means pursuing relationships that honor God and reflect His love, rather than seeking instant gratification or following the patterns of the world.

One of the primary ways that purity of heart manifests in the waiting period is through sexual purity. In a culture that often promotes sexual freedom and experimentation, the biblical call to abstain from sexual immorality until marriage can seem outdated or restrictive. However, Scripture is clear that sexual purity is an essential aspect of holiness and a reflection of our commitment to God.

1 Thessalonians 4:3-5 states, *"For this is the will of God, your sanctification: that you abstain from sexual immorality; that each one of you know how to control his own body in holiness and honor, not in the passion of lust like the Gentiles who do not know God."* Here, Paul emphasizes that sexual purity is not just about following rules; it is about honoring God with our bodies and living in a way that is distinct from those who do not know Him.

Sexual purity is not only about abstaining from physical acts but also about guarding our hearts and minds from impure thoughts and desires. Jesus teaches in Matthew 5:27-28, *"You have heard that it was said, 'You shall not commit adultery.' But I say to you that everyone who looks at a woman with lustful intent has already committed adultery with her in his heart."* This teaching underscores the importance of maintaining purity not only in our actions but also in our inner lives.

Maintaining purity while waiting for love also involves cultivating healthy boundaries in our relationships. This includes setting physical, emotional, and spiritual boundaries that protect both ourselves and our potential partners from falling into temptation. It means being intentional about the way we interact with others, avoiding situations that could lead to compromise, and seeking accountability from trusted friends or mentors.

However, purity of heart is not just about avoiding sin; it is also about actively pursuing holiness. This means seeking to grow in our relationship with God, spending time in prayer and Scripture, and allowing the Holy Spirit to transform us from the inside out. It means seeking to love others with a pure and sincere heart, free from selfishness, manipulation, or ulterior motives.

The Challenges of Maintaining Purity

MAINTAINING PURITY of heart while waiting for love is not without its challenges. In a world that often celebrates instant gratification and self-indulgence, the call to purity can feel like an uphill battle. We face pressures from society, media, and even our own desires that can make it difficult to stay on the path of purity.

One of the biggest challenges is the temptation to compromise. When we are waiting for love, it can be easy to lower our standards or settle for less than God's best. We may be tempted to enter into a relationship that does not honor God, to engage in behaviors that go against our values, or to rationalize our actions in the name of love.

For example, we might justify spending time alone with someone we are attracted to, even if it leads to physical temptation. We might downplay the importance of sexual purity, convincing ourselves that it is not a big deal or that we can handle it. Or we might engage in emotional intimacy with someone who is not committed to us, allowing our hearts to become entangled in ways that are not honoring to God.

Another challenge is the influence of the culture around us. We live in a society that often glorifies sexual freedom, casual relationships, and self-gratification. Media, entertainment, and social networks bombard us with messages that promote these values, making it difficult to stay focused on God's standard of purity.

In addition, we may face pressure from peers or even from within the Christian community to conform to worldly standards. We might feel isolated or out of step with others who do not share our commitment to purity. This can lead to feelings of loneliness, frustration, or doubt, causing us to question whether it is worth it to maintain our purity.

The battle for purity is not just external; it is also internal. Our own hearts can be a source of temptation, as we struggle with desires, thoughts, and emotions that pull us away from God. The Bible acknowledges this struggle in James 1:14-15: *"But each person is tempted when he is lured and enticed by his own desire. Then desire when it has conceived gives birth to sin, and sin when it is fully grown brings forth death."* The progression from desire to sin to spiritual death highlights the importance of addressing the root issues in our hearts.

However, while the challenges are real, they are not insurmountable. God has given us the tools we need to overcome temptation and maintain purity of heart. Through the power of the Holy Spirit, the guidance of Scripture, and the support of a faithful community, we can stand firm in our commitment to purity and experience the blessings that come from waiting with a clean and sincere heart.

The Role of Grace in Purity

MAINTAINING PURITY of heart is not something we can do on our own. It requires the grace of God working in our lives, empowering us to live in a way that honors Him. Grace is not just a concept; it is a divine gift that enables us to overcome sin, grow in holiness, and reflect the character of Christ.

In Titus 2:11-14, Paul writes about the transformative power of grace: *"For the grace of God has appeared, bringing salvation for all people, training us to renounce ungodliness and worldly passions, and to live self-controlled, upright, and godly lives in the present age, waiting for our blessed hope, the appearing of the glory of our great God and Savior Jesus Christ, who gave himself for us to redeem us from all lawlessness and to purify for himself a people for his own possession who are zealous for good works."* This passage highlights how grace not only brings us salvation but also trains us to live in purity and godliness.

Grace empowers us to say no to ungodliness and worldly passions, and it trains us to live self-controlled, upright, and godly lives. It is through grace that we are able to resist temptation, to set healthy boundaries, and to pursue purity in our relationships. Grace is not a license to sin but a power that enables us to overcome sin and to walk in the freedom that Christ has given us.

Moreover, grace is also at work in our hearts, transforming us from the inside out. In Ezekiel 36:26, God promises, *"And I will give you a new heart, and a new spirit I will put within you. And I will remove the heart of stone from your flesh and give you a heart of flesh."* This is the work of grace in our lives, softening our hearts, renewing our desires, and aligning our will with God's will.

As we wait for love, we can rely on God's grace to help us maintain purity of heart. We can turn to Him in prayer, asking for His strength and guidance, and trusting that He will provide the grace we need to stay faithful. We can also extend grace to ourselves and others, recognizing that we are all in the process of growth and that God's grace is sufficient to cover our weaknesses and failures.

The Blessings of a Pure Heart

JESUS' PROMISE IN MATTHEW 5:8, *"Blessed are the pure in heart, for they shall see God,"* offers a glimpse into the profound blessings that come from maintaining purity. The pure in heart are not only blessed with the ability to see God but also experience His presence, guidance, and favor in their lives.

One of the blessings of a pure heart is a deeper intimacy with God. When our hearts are pure, we are able to approach God with confidence, knowing that there is nothing hindering our relationship with Him. We can experience His love, peace, and joy in greater measure, and we can hear His voice more clearly.

Psalm 24:3-4 echoes this truth: *"Who shall ascend the hill of the Lord? And who shall stand in his holy place? He who has clean hands and a pure heart, who does not lift up his soul to what is false and does not swear deceitfully."* Purity of heart enables us to draw near to God, to stand in His presence, and to experience the fullness of life that He offers.

In the context of relationships, a pure heart also leads to healthier, more fulfilling relationships. When we maintain purity, we are able to build relationships on a foundation of trust, respect, and mutual honor. We are free from the guilt, shame, and complications that often come with compromise, and we can enter into relationships with a clear conscience.

Moreover, a pure heart allows us to love others with a genuine and selfless love. 1 Timothy 1:5 reminds us that *"The aim of our charge is love that issues from a pure heart and a good conscience and a sincere faith."* Purity of heart enables us to love others as Christ loves us, with a love that is patient, kind, and free from selfishness or manipulation.

Finally, a pure heart positions us to receive God's best for our lives. When we wait for love with a pure heart, we are trusting that God will bring the right person into our lives at the right time. We are aligning ourselves with His will and His timing, and we can be confident that He will honor our commitment to purity by blessing us with a relationship that reflects His love and goodness.

Practical Steps to Cultivate Purity of Heart

MAINTAINING PURITY of heart while waiting for love requires intentionality and commitment. Here are some practical steps to help you cultivate purity in your relationships:

1. Guard Your Heart: Proverbs 4:23 advises, *"Keep your heart with all vigilance, for from it flow the springs of life."* Be intentional about what you allow into your heart, including the media you consume, the conversations you engage in, and the relationships you pursue. Protect your heart from influences that can lead you away from God and His will for your life.

2. Set Boundaries: Establish clear physical, emotional, and spiritual boundaries in your relationships. Communicate your boundaries with your partner and seek accountability from trusted friends or mentors. Boundaries are not restrictions; they are safeguards that protect your heart and honor God.

3. Pursue Holiness: 1 Peter 1:15-16 calls us to be holy in all our conduct, as God is holy. Seek to grow in your relationship with God through prayer, Scripture reading, and worship. Allow the Holy Spirit to transform your heart and align your desires with God's will.

4. Seek Accountability: Surround yourself with a community of believers who share your commitment to purity. Seek accountability from trusted

friends, mentors, or small groups who can support you, pray for you, and help you stay on the path of purity.

5. Renew Your Mind: Romans 12:2 encourages us to *"be transformed by the renewal of your mind."* Be intentional about renewing your mind with God's truth. Replace negative or impure thoughts with Scripture, and meditate on verses that reinforce your commitment to purity.

6. Flee Temptation: 2 Timothy 2:22 advises us to *"flee youthful passions and pursue righteousness, faith, love, and peace."* When faced with temptation, don't try to resist it on your own—flee from it. Remove yourself from situations that can lead to compromise and seek God's strength to overcome temptation.

7. Practice Self-Control: Galatians 5:22-23 lists self-control as one of the fruits of the Spirit. Cultivate self-control in your thoughts, words, and actions. This might involve practicing self-discipline, such as limiting physical affection in a relationship, or being mindful of the media you consume.

8. Pray for Purity: Ask God to purify your heart and to help you maintain purity in your relationships. Prayer is a powerful tool that connects us with God's grace and strength. Pray regularly for God's guidance, wisdom, and protection as you navigate the challenges of maintaining purity.

Conclusion: A Heart Prepared for Love

PURITY OF HEART IS not just about following rules or avoiding sin; it is about preparing our hearts to receive God's best for our lives. When we maintain purity while waiting for love, we are positioning ourselves to experience the fullness of God's blessings in our relationships.

Matthew 5:8, *"Blessed are the pure in heart, for they shall see God,"* reminds us that purity is not only a call to holiness but also a pathway to deeper intimacy with God. As we pursue purity of heart, we are invited to see God more clearly, to experience His presence more fully, and to walk in the light of His truth.

In the context of relationships, maintaining purity of heart allows us to build relationships that reflect God's love, honor His design for marriage, and bring glory to His name. It enables us to wait for love with a clean and sincere heart, trusting that God will bring the right person into our lives at the right time.

As you wait for love, may you be encouraged to pursue purity of heart with all diligence. May you guard your heart, set healthy boundaries, and seek God's grace to help you overcome the challenges of maintaining purity. And may you be blessed with the joy and fulfillment that come from waiting with a heart that is pure, sincere, and fully devoted to God.

Chapter 4: The Power of Prayer

Theological Reflection: Reflect on the role of prayer in seeking and waiting for love. Use Philippians 4:6-7 to illustrate how prayer brings peace and aligns our desires with God's will.

Introduction: The Lifeline of Prayer

IN THE JOURNEY OF SEEKING and waiting for love, prayer stands as a crucial pillar, offering guidance, comfort, and a deep connection with God. It is through prayer that we open our hearts to God, share our deepest desires, and seek His will for our lives. In Philippians 4:6-7, the Apostle Paul provides profound insight into the transformative power of prayer: *"Do not be anxious about anything, but in everything by prayer and supplication with thanksgiving let your requests be made known to God. And the peace of God, which surpasses all understanding, will guard your hearts and your minds in Christ Jesus."*

These verses encapsulate the essence of prayer in the Christian life, particularly in the context of love and relationships. They remind us that prayer is not just about asking God for what we want but about aligning our hearts with His will, finding peace in His presence, and trusting in His perfect timing.

This chapter explores the power of prayer in the context of seeking and waiting for love. We will delve into the biblical understanding of prayer, the role it plays in aligning our desires with God's will, and the peace that comes from surrendering our hopes and fears to Him. Through the lens of Philippians

4:6-7, we will examine how prayer can transform our hearts, guide our decisions, and lead us to the love that God has prepared for us.

The Biblical Foundation of Prayer

PRAYER IS A CENTRAL theme throughout the Bible, serving as the primary means of communication between God and His people. From the earliest stories in the Old Testament to the teachings of Jesus in the New Testament, prayer is portrayed as a powerful and essential practice for believers.

In the Old Testament, we see examples of prayer as a means of seeking God's guidance, expressing gratitude, and interceding for others. Abraham, Moses, David, and the prophets all engaged in deep, heartfelt prayers that shaped their lives and the course of history. For instance, Moses' prayer in Exodus 33:13 reflects his desire for God's guidance: *"Now therefore, if I have found favor in your sight, please show me now your ways, that I may know you in order to find favor in your sight."* This prayer reveals the intimate relationship between Moses and God, where Moses seeks not only direction but also a deeper understanding of God's character.

The Psalms, many of which were written by David, are filled with prayers of praise, lament, thanksgiving, and supplication. Psalm 86:6-7 captures the essence of prayer as a plea for help: *"Give ear, O Lord, to my prayer; listen to my plea for grace. In the day of my trouble I call upon you, for you answer me."* David's prayers demonstrate a deep reliance on God in both times of joy and times of distress.

In the New Testament, Jesus Himself models the importance of prayer. Throughout His ministry, Jesus frequently withdrew to solitary places to pray, seeking communion with the Father and strength for His mission. In the Garden of Gethsemane, Jesus' prayer in Matthew 26:39 reflects His submission to God's will: *"My Father, if it be possible, let this cup pass from me; nevertheless, not as I will, but as you will."* This prayer exemplifies the ultimate act of surrender, where Jesus aligns His desires with the Father's will, even in the face of immense suffering.

The Lord's Prayer, given by Jesus in Matthew 6:9-13, provides a model for how we should approach God in prayer. It encompasses praise, submission to God's will, requests for daily needs, forgiveness, and protection from temptation. The Lord's Prayer reminds us that prayer is not just about presenting our requests but about seeking God's kingdom and His righteousness in all aspects of our lives.

Prayer in the Context of Seeking Love

WHEN IT COMES TO SEEKING love, prayer plays a vital role in shaping our desires, guiding our decisions, and preparing our hearts for the relationships God has planned for us. The process of seeking love can be filled with uncertainty, longing, and sometimes anxiety. It is during these times that prayer becomes our lifeline, connecting us with the God who knows us intimately and desires the best for us.

One of the primary ways that prayer influences our journey in seeking love is by aligning our desires with God's will. As human beings, our desires are often influenced by a variety of factors, including cultural expectations, personal preferences, and even past experiences. While it is natural to have desires and hopes for a future relationship, it is essential to submit these desires to God in prayer, asking Him to purify and align them with His will.

James 4:3 warns us about the dangers of praying with selfish motives: *"You ask and do not receive, because you ask wrongly, to spend it on your passions."* This verse reminds us that our prayers must be guided by a desire to honor God rather than simply fulfill our own passions. When we seek love through prayer, we are inviting God to shape our desires according to His perfect plan.

Praying for guidance in seeking love also helps us discern God's will for our lives. Proverbs 3:5-6 encourages us to *"Trust in the Lord with all your heart, and do not lean on your own understanding. In all your ways acknowledge him, and he will make straight your paths."* When we pray for guidance, we are acknowledging that we need God's wisdom to make decisions that align with His will. This might involve asking for clarity in discerning whether a particular relationship is God's best for us or seeking wisdom in navigating the challenges of dating and courtship.

Prayer also prepares our hearts for the love that God has planned for us. In the waiting period, prayer can be a powerful tool for personal growth and spiritual development. As we pray, we invite God to work in our hearts, molding us into the people He has called us to be. This might involve healing from past wounds, developing godly character traits, or growing in patience and trust.

Ephesians 3:16-19 offers a beautiful prayer for spiritual strength and growth: *"That according to the riches of his glory he may grant you to be strengthened with power through his Spirit in your inner being, so that Christ may dwell in your hearts through faith—that you, being rooted and grounded in love, may have strength to comprehend with all the saints what is the breadth and length and height and depth, and to know the love of Christ that surpasses knowledge, that you may be filled with all the fullness of God."* This prayer reflects the transformative power of God's love in our lives and the importance of being rooted and grounded in that love as we seek a future relationship.

The Role of Prayer in Waiting for Love

WAITING FOR LOVE CAN be one of the most challenging and faith-stretching experiences in a believer's life. The period of waiting often brings with it feelings of loneliness, impatience, and sometimes even doubt. However, it is precisely in this season of waiting that prayer becomes a source of strength, comfort, and peace.

Philippians 4:6-7 offers a powerful reminder of the role of prayer in overcoming anxiety and finding peace in God's presence: *"Do not be anxious about anything, but in everything by prayer and supplication with thanksgiving let your requests be made known to God. And the peace of God, which surpasses all understanding, will guard your hearts and your minds in Christ Jesus."* These verses highlight the importance of bringing our anxieties, fears, and desires to God in prayer and trusting that He will provide the peace that transcends human understanding.

When we pray during the waiting period, we are actively surrendering our worries and concerns to God. Instead of allowing anxiety to take root in our hearts, we choose to trust that God is in control and that His timing is perfect. This act of surrender is not passive; it is a deliberate choice to place our trust in God's sovereignty and goodness.

Prayer also helps us cultivate a spirit of thanksgiving, even in the midst of waiting. Paul encourages us to present our requests to God with thanksgiving, recognizing that God is faithful and that He has already blessed us in countless ways. When we approach God with a thankful heart, we shift our focus from what we lack to what we already have, and we become more attuned to God's presence and provision in our lives.

Psalm 100:4-5 emphasizes the importance of entering God's presence with thanksgiving: *"Enter his gates with thanksgiving, and his courts with praise! Give thanks to him; bless his name! For the Lord is good; his steadfast love endures forever, and his faithfulness to all generations."* Thanksgiving is a powerful antidote to anxiety, as it reminds us of God's goodness and faithfulness throughout our lives.

In addition to bringing peace, prayer also strengthens our faith during the waiting period. Hebrews 11:1 defines faith as *"the assurance of things hoped for, the conviction of things not seen."* Prayer is an expression of our faith, as we trust that God is working behind the scenes, even when we cannot see the outcome. Through prayer, we are reminded that God is faithful to His promises and that He will fulfill His plans for our lives in His perfect timing.

Waiting for love also provides an opportunity to deepen our relationship with God through prayer. Instead of viewing the waiting period as wasted time, we can see it as a season of preparation and growth. As we spend time in prayer, we draw closer to God, and our hearts become more aligned with His will. We learn to rely on His strength, seek His wisdom, and find our ultimate satisfaction in Him.

Psalm 27:14 encourages us to *"Wait for the Lord; be strong, and let your heart take courage; wait for the Lord!"* This verse reminds us that waiting is not passive but requires strength, courage, and a deep trust in God's faithfulness. Through prayer, we can find the strength to persevere in the waiting period, knowing that God is working all things together for our good.

Aligning Our Desires with God's Will Through

Prayer

ONE OF THE MOST POWERFUL aspects of prayer is its ability to align our desires with God's will. As we pray, we invite God to shape and refine our desires, transforming them from self-centered wishes to God-centered aspirations. This process of alignment is essential, especially in the context of seeking and waiting for love.

Romans 12:2 speaks to the importance of aligning our minds and hearts with God's will: *"Do not be conformed to this world, but be transformed by the renewal of your mind, that by testing you may discern what is the will of God, what is good and acceptable and perfect."* Prayer plays a crucial role in this transformation, as it allows us to submit our desires to God and seek His guidance in all aspects of our lives.

In the context of relationships, aligning our desires with God's will means surrendering our preferences, timelines, and expectations to Him. It involves asking God to reveal His will for our love lives and trusting that His plans are far better than anything we could imagine. This might mean letting go of a relationship that is not God's best for us or waiting patiently for the right person to come into our lives.

When we pray for God's will to be done in our relationships, we are expressing our trust in His sovereignty and goodness. We are acknowledging that He knows what is best for us, even when we do not fully understand His plans. This act of surrender is an essential aspect of faith, as it requires us to let go of control and place our trust in God's perfect wisdom.

Jesus models this type of surrender in His prayer in the Garden of Gethsemane, as recorded in Matthew 26:39: *"My Father, if it be possible, let this cup pass from me; nevertheless, not as I will, but as you will."* Jesus' prayer reflects His willingness to submit to the Father's will, even in the face of immense suffering. This prayer serves as a powerful example of how we should approach God in prayer, with a heart that is willing to submit to His will, even when it requires sacrifice.

As we align our desires with God's will through prayer, we also begin to experience a greater sense of peace and contentment. When our desires are in harmony with God's plan, we are no longer driven by impatience, fear, or anxiety. Instead, we can rest in the assurance that God is in control and that He will fulfill His promises to us in His perfect timing.

Philippians 4:6-7 reminds us of the peace that comes from aligning our desires with God's will: *"And the peace of God, which surpasses all understanding, will guard your hearts and your minds in Christ Jesus."* This peace is not dependent on our circumstances or the fulfillment of our desires; it is a gift from God that transcends our understanding and guards our hearts and minds in Christ.

Aligning our desires with God's will also frees us from the pressure to conform to the expectations of the world. In a culture that often equates love with physical attraction, status, or material success, it can be easy to lose sight of God's design for relationships. However, when we seek God's will through prayer, we are reminded that true love is rooted in commitment, selflessness, and a desire to honor God.

1 Corinthians 13:4-7 offers a biblical definition of love that contrasts sharply with the world's definition: *"Love is patient and kind; love does not envy or boast; it is not arrogant or rude. It does not insist on its own way; it is not irritable or resentful; it does not rejoice at wrongdoing, but rejoices with the truth. Love bears all things, believes all things, hopes all things, endures all things."* As we pray for God's will in our relationships, we can ask Him to cultivate these qualities of love in our hearts and to lead us into relationships that reflect His character.

The Transformative Power of Prayer

PRAYER IS NOT ONLY a means of communication with God; it is also a powerful tool for transformation. As we pray, God works in our hearts, renewing our minds, shaping our character, and aligning our lives with His purposes. This transformative power of prayer is especially evident in the context of seeking and waiting for love.

One of the ways that prayer transforms us is by deepening our dependence on God. When we bring our desires, anxieties, and hopes to God in prayer, we are acknowledging our need for His guidance and strength. This dependence on God fosters a deeper relationship with Him, as we learn to trust Him more fully and rely on His grace in every aspect of our lives.

Psalm 62:8 encourages us to pour out our hearts to God: *"Trust in him at all times, O people; pour out your heart before him; God is a refuge for us."* Prayer allows us to be honest and vulnerable before God, sharing our deepest longings and fears, and finding refuge in His presence. As we pour out our hearts to God, He meets us with His love, comfort, and peace, transforming our hearts and minds.

Prayer also transforms our perspective, helping us to see our circumstances through the lens of God's sovereignty and goodness. When we are faced with uncertainty or disappointment in our relationships, it can be easy to become discouraged or lose hope. However, through prayer, we are reminded that God is in control and that He is working all things together for our good.

Romans 8:28 offers this assurance: *"And we know that for those who love God all things work together for good, for those who are called according to his purpose."* Prayer helps us to hold onto this truth, even when our circumstances seem to suggest otherwise. It shifts our focus from our immediate concerns to God's eternal purposes, allowing us to trust in His plan even when we cannot see the outcome.

Another way that prayer transforms us is by cultivating patience and perseverance. Waiting for love can be a long and difficult journey, but prayer helps us to endure the waiting period with grace and faith. Through prayer, we are reminded that God's timing is perfect and that He is faithful to fulfill His promises.

James 1:2-4 speaks to the importance of perseverance in the Christian life: *"Count it all joy, my brothers, when you meet trials of various kinds, for you know that the testing of your faith produces steadfastness. And let steadfastness have its full effect, that you may be perfect and complete, lacking in nothing."* Prayer strengthens our faith and helps us to persevere through the trials and challenges of waiting, knowing that God is at work in our lives.

Prayer also has the power to heal and restore. If we have experienced past hurts or disappointments in relationships, prayer can be a source of healing and renewal. As we bring our wounds to God in prayer, He offers us His comfort, forgiveness, and grace, allowing us to move forward with a renewed sense of hope and trust in His plan.

Psalm 147:3 offers this promise of healing: *"He heals the brokenhearted and binds up their wounds."* Prayer invites God to enter into our pain and bring healing to our hearts. It allows us to release our burdens to Him and to trust that He will bring restoration and renewal to our lives.

Practical Steps for Cultivating a Life of Prayer

CULTIVATING A LIFE of prayer is essential for seeking and waiting for love with faith and trust in God. Here are some practical steps to help you develop a consistent and meaningful prayer life:

1. Set Aside Regular Time for Prayer: Establish a daily routine for prayer, setting aside specific times to spend with God. Whether it's in the morning, during a lunch break, or before bed, making prayer a regular part of your day helps to cultivate a habit of seeking God and aligning your heart with His will.

2. Create a Prayer Journal: Consider keeping a prayer journal where you can write down your prayers, thoughts, and reflections. This can be a helpful way to organize your prayers, track your spiritual growth, and reflect on how God has answered your prayers over time.

3. Pray with Scripture: Use Scripture as a guide for your prayers, allowing God's Word to shape and inform your requests. Praying with Scripture helps to align your desires with God's will and to deepen your understanding of His promises.

4. Incorporate Thanksgiving and Praise: Begin your prayers with thanksgiving and praise, acknowledging God's goodness and faithfulness in your life. This helps to shift your focus from your concerns to God's character and to cultivate a heart of gratitude.

5. Be Honest and Vulnerable: Approach God with honesty and vulnerability, sharing your deepest desires, fears, and hopes. Remember that God knows your heart and desires to meet you in your place of need.

6. Seek God's Will: Make it a priority to seek God's will in your prayers, asking Him to align your desires with His purposes. This might involve surrendering your own preferences and trusting that God's plans are better than your own.

7. Pray for Others: In addition to praying for your own needs, take time to pray for others, including friends, family, and those in your community. Praying for others helps to cultivate a heart of compassion and to keep your focus on God's work in the lives of those around you.

8. Pray Continually: Develop the habit of continual prayer, offering up short prayers throughout the day as you go about your daily activities. This helps to keep you connected with God and to cultivate an attitude of dependence on Him.

Conclusion: The Peace and Power of Prayer

PRAYER IS A POWERFUL and transformative practice that connects us with the God who loves us and desires the best for our lives. In the journey of seeking and waiting for love, prayer serves as a source of strength, guidance, and peace, helping us to align our desires with God's will and to trust in His perfect timing.

Philippians 4:6-7 offers a beautiful promise of the peace that comes from prayer: "Do not be anxious about anything, but in everything by prayer and supplication with thanksgiving let your requests be made known to God. And the peace of God, which surpasses all understanding, will guard your hearts and your minds in Christ Jesus." This peace is not dependent on our circumstances or the fulfillment of our desires; it is a gift from God that transcends human understanding and guards our hearts and minds in Christ.

As you seek and wait for love, may you be encouraged to cultivate a life of prayer, trusting that God is at work in your life and that He has a good and perfect plan for you. May you find peace in His presence, strength in His promises, and joy in the journey of following Him. And may your prayers lead you to the love that God has prepared for you—a love that reflects His character and brings glory to His name.

Chapter 5: The Role of Friendship in Love

Theological Reflection: Discuss the importance of building a strong foundation of friendship in a romantic relationship. Reference Proverbs 17:17, which speaks to the value of a friend, and relate it to love that is worth waiting for.

Introduction: The Cornerstone of Love

IN THE REALM OF ROMANTIC relationships, one often hears the phrase, "marry your best friend." This saying points to a profound truth: the strongest and most enduring romantic relationships are built on the foundation of genuine friendship. Friendship brings with it trust, understanding, shared values, and mutual respect—qualities that are essential for a healthy, lasting relationship. As Proverbs 17:17 wisely states, *"A friend loves at all times, and a brother is born for adversity."* This verse captures the essence of true friendship—a relationship characterized by steadfast love and unwavering support, even in the face of challenges.

In this chapter, we will explore the role of friendship in romantic relationships, highlighting how a strong foundation of friendship can lead to a love that is worth waiting for. We will delve into the biblical understanding of friendship, the qualities that define a godly friendship, and how these qualities contribute to a thriving romantic relationship. Through the lens of Proverbs 17:17, we will reflect on the value of friendship in love and how cultivating this bond can lead to a deeper, more meaningful connection with our partner.

The Biblical Concept of Friendship

FRIENDSHIP IS A RECURRING theme throughout the Bible, where it is often portrayed as a vital component of human relationships. The Bible presents friendship as a bond of mutual affection, trust, and loyalty, a relationship that reflects the love and faithfulness of God. In a world where friendships can sometimes be superficial or transactional, the biblical concept of friendship offers a deeper, more meaningful vision of what it means to be a true friend.

One of the most famous examples of friendship in the Bible is the relationship between David and Jonathan. Their friendship is described in 1 Samuel 18:1-4: *"The soul of Jonathan was knit to the soul of David, and Jonathan loved him as his own soul. And Saul took him that day and would not let him return to his father's house. Then Jonathan made a covenant with David, because he loved him as his own soul. And Jonathan stripped himself of the robe that was on him and gave it to David, and his armor, and even his sword and his bow and his belt."* Jonathan's selfless love and loyalty to David, even at the cost of his own future as king, exemplify the depth and strength of true friendship.

The book of Proverbs also offers numerous insights into the nature of friendship. Proverbs 18:24, for example, contrasts shallow friendships with deep, abiding ones: *"A man of many companions may come to ruin, but there is a friend who sticks closer than a brother."* This verse highlights the importance of quality over quantity in friendships, emphasizing that true friendship involves commitment and loyalty, qualities that mirror the steadfast love of God.

Jesus Himself exemplified the ultimate model of friendship. In John 15:13-15, He tells His disciples, *"Greater love has no one than this, that someone lay down his life for his friends. You are my friends if you do what I command you. No longer do I call you servants, for the servant does not know what his master is doing; but I have called you friends, for all that I have heard from my Father I have made known to you."* Here, Jesus defines friendship as sacrificial love, rooted in mutual knowledge and obedience to God's will. His willingness to lay down His life for His friends demonstrates the profound depth of His love and commitment to those He calls His own.

The biblical concept of friendship, therefore, is not merely about companionship or shared interests; it is about deep, abiding love, loyalty, and mutual respect. These qualities are foundational to any relationship, but they take on special significance in the context of a romantic relationship, where friendship serves as the bedrock upon which love is built.

The Role of Friendship in Romantic Relationships

IN ROMANTIC RELATIONSHIPS, friendship plays a crucial role in building a strong, enduring bond between partners. While physical attraction and emotional connection are often the initial sparks that ignite a romantic relationship, it is friendship that sustains and deepens the relationship over time. A romantic relationship that lacks a foundation of friendship may struggle to withstand the challenges and trials that inevitably arise in any partnership.

Friendship in a romantic relationship is characterized by several key qualities: trust, communication, shared values, mutual respect, and a commitment to one another's well-being. These qualities are not only essential for a healthy friendship but also for a thriving romantic relationship.

Trust is the cornerstone of both friendship and love. In a romantic relationship, trust allows partners to be vulnerable with one another, to share their deepest thoughts, feelings, and fears, knowing that they will be met with understanding and compassion. Trust is built over time, through consistent, reliable actions and open, honest communication. When a romantic relationship is rooted in friendship, trust naturally flourishes, creating a safe and secure environment for both partners.

Communication is another vital component of friendship in a romantic relationship. Good friends communicate openly and honestly with one another, sharing their thoughts and feelings without fear of judgment. In a romantic relationship, effective communication is essential for resolving conflicts, expressing love and appreciation, and deepening the connection between partners. When a romantic relationship is founded on friendship, communication becomes easier and more natural, as partners already have a foundation of understanding and trust.

Shared values are also a key element of friendship in a romantic relationship. Friends often share similar beliefs, goals, and priorities, which create a sense of unity and purpose in the relationship. In a romantic relationship, shared values provide a common foundation upon which partners can build their lives together. When a romantic relationship is rooted in friendship, partners are more likely to share common values and goals, which helps to create a strong, cohesive partnership.

Mutual respect is another hallmark of friendship in a romantic relationship. True friends respect one another's opinions, boundaries, and individuality, and they seek to uplift and support one another. In a romantic relationship, mutual respect is essential for maintaining a healthy, balanced partnership. When a romantic relationship is built on friendship, partners are more likely to treat one another with kindness, respect, and consideration, creating a harmonious and fulfilling relationship.

Finally, **commitment to one another's well-being** is a defining characteristic of friendship in a romantic relationship. True friends are invested in each other's happiness and success, and they are willing to make sacrifices for the sake of the relationship. In a romantic relationship, this commitment translates into a willingness to prioritize the needs of the relationship, to support one another through difficult times, and to work together to overcome challenges. When a romantic relationship is founded on friendship, this commitment becomes a natural extension of the love and care that partners have for one another.

Proverbs 17:17 and the Value of Friendship in Love

PROVERBS 17:17 OFFERS a profound insight into the value of friendship in love: *"A friend loves at all times, and a brother is born for adversity."* This verse highlights the enduring nature of true friendship, which is characterized by constant, unwavering love, even in the face of adversity. In the context of a romantic relationship, this type of steadfast friendship serves as the foundation for a love that can withstand the tests of time.

"A friend loves at all times." The first part of this verse emphasizes the constancy of a true friend's love. In a romantic relationship, this translates into a commitment to love and support one another through all seasons of life—whether in times of joy or sorrow, success or failure, health or sickness. A romantic relationship that is rooted in friendship is marked by this kind of steadfast love, which does not waver based on changing circumstances.

In a culture that often prioritizes instant gratification and fleeting emotions, the idea of loving "at all times" can seem countercultural. However, true love—love that is worth waiting for—is not based on temporary feelings or external factors; it is grounded in a deep, abiding friendship that endures through all of life's ups and downs. This kind of love is not dependent on circumstances but is rooted in the character and commitment of both partners.

"A brother is born for adversity." The second part of this verse speaks to the role of a friend (or in this case, a "brother") in times of difficulty. Just as a brother is there to support and stand by us during challenging times, a true friend in a romantic relationship is someone who will walk with us through adversity. This type of friendship provides a source of strength and encouragement when faced with trials, whether they are personal, relational, or external challenges.

In a romantic relationship, adversity is inevitable. There will be times of conflict, misunderstanding, and hardship. However, when a relationship is built on the foundation of friendship, partners are better equipped to navigate these challenges together. They can draw on the deep reservoir of trust, communication, and mutual respect that has been established through their friendship, allowing them to face adversity with unity and resilience.

Moreover, a romantic relationship that is rooted in friendship allows partners to truly know and understand one another. They have taken the time to build a strong foundation of trust and communication, which enables them to navigate conflicts with empathy and patience. This kind of relationship is not just about romantic love but about a deep, enduring bond that can withstand the tests of time and adversity.

The Blessings of a Friendship-Based Relationship

BUILDING A ROMANTIC relationship on the foundation of friendship brings with it numerous blessings, both for the individuals involved and for the relationship as a whole. These blessings include emotional security, personal growth, mutual support, and a deeper, more enduring love.

Emotional Security: One of the greatest blessings of a friendship-based relationship is the sense of emotional security that it provides. When partners have established a strong foundation of friendship, they are able to trust one another fully and feel safe in the relationship. This emotional security allows them to be vulnerable with one another, to share their deepest thoughts and feelings, and to be their authentic selves without fear of judgment or rejection.

In a friendship-based relationship, partners are not constantly seeking validation or approval from one another. Instead, they find security in the knowledge that they are loved and accepted for who they are. This emotional security creates a stable and nurturing environment in which love can flourish.

Personal Growth: Another blessing of a friendship-based relationship is the opportunity for personal growth. True friends challenge and inspire one another to become the best versions of themselves. In a romantic relationship, this means that partners encourage one another to pursue their goals, develop their talents, and grow in their relationship with God.

A friendship-based relationship provides a supportive environment in which both partners can grow and mature, both individually and as a couple. They are able to challenge one another in love, offering constructive feedback and encouragement that fosters personal growth. This kind of relationship is not static but dynamic, as both partners continue to evolve and grow together.

Mutual Support: Friendship in a romantic relationship also brings the blessing of mutual support. True friends are there for one another in both good times and bad, offering a listening ear, a comforting presence, and practical help when needed. In a romantic relationship, this mutual support becomes a source of strength and stability.

Partners in a friendship-based relationship are committed to supporting one another through all of life's challenges, whether they are facing personal struggles, family issues, or external pressures. They are able to rely on one another for emotional and practical support, knowing that they are not alone in facing life's difficulties.

A Deeper, More Enduring Love: Perhaps the greatest blessing of a friendship-based relationship is the deep, enduring love that it fosters. When love is built on the foundation of friendship, it is not based solely on physical attraction or fleeting emotions but on a deep, abiding connection that grows stronger over time.

A friendship-based love is characterized by mutual respect, trust, and commitment. It is a love that endures through all of life's seasons, whether in times of joy or sorrow, success or failure. This kind of love is not dependent on external factors but is rooted in the character and commitment of both partners.

In a friendship-based relationship, love is not just a feeling but a choice—an intentional commitment to love and support one another, even when it is difficult. This kind of love is worth waiting for, as it brings with it the promise of a deep, meaningful connection that can withstand the tests of time.

Cultivating Friendship in a Romantic Relationship

BUILDING A STRONG FOUNDATION of friendship in a romantic relationship requires intentional effort and commitment from both partners. Here are some practical steps for cultivating friendship in your romantic relationship:

1. Prioritize Communication: Communication is the lifeblood of any relationship, and it is especially important in a friendship-based relationship. Make time to talk with your partner regularly, sharing your thoughts, feelings, and experiences. Listen actively and empathetically, and be open and honest in your communication. Good communication builds trust and understanding, which are essential for a strong friendship.

2. Spend Quality Time Together: Friendship is built through shared experiences and quality time together. Make time to engage in activities that you both enjoy, whether it is going for a walk, cooking a meal together, or simply sitting and talking. Prioritize spending time together, even in the midst of busy schedules, and make an effort to create meaningful memories together.

3. Support Each Other's Goals: True friends support one another's goals and aspirations, and this is just as important in a romantic relationship. Take an interest in your partner's dreams and goals, and offer your support and encouragement. Celebrate each other's successes and offer a listening ear and a shoulder to lean on during times of difficulty.

4. Be Patient and Forgiving: No relationship is without its challenges, and it is important to approach these challenges with patience and forgiveness. Be patient with your partner's imperfections and mistakes, and be quick to offer

forgiveness when conflicts arise. Remember that friendship is about loving and supporting one another, even when it is difficult.

5. Cultivate Shared Values and Interests: Shared values and interests are the foundation of any strong friendship. Take the time to explore and cultivate the values and interests that you share with your partner. This might involve engaging in activities that you both enjoy, discussing your beliefs and priorities, or working together on a common goal.

6. Practice Selflessness: True friendship is characterized by selflessness and a willingness to put the needs of the other person first. In a romantic relationship, this means being willing to make sacrifices for the sake of the relationship, to prioritize your partner's well-being, and to seek their happiness above your own.

7. Seek God Together: One of the most important aspects of a friendship-based relationship is a shared commitment to seeking God together. Make time to pray together, read Scripture together, and encourage one another in your walk with God. A relationship that is rooted in a shared faith is stronger and more resilient, as it is built on the foundation of God's love and truth.

Conclusion: Love Worth Waiting For

THE ROLE OF FRIENDSHIP in love cannot be overstated. A romantic relationship that is built on the foundation of friendship is stronger, deeper, and more enduring. It is a love that is characterized by trust, communication, shared values, mutual respect, and a commitment to one another's well-being.

Proverbs 17:17 reminds us of the value of true friendship: *"A friend loves at all times, and a brother is born for adversity."* This verse encapsulates the essence of a friendship-based relationship—a relationship that is marked by steadfast love, unwavering support, and a deep, abiding connection that can withstand the tests of time.

As you seek and wait for love, may you be encouraged to prioritize friendship in your romantic relationships. May you take the time to build a strong foundation of trust, communication, shared values, and mutual respect. And may you find a love that is worth waiting for—a love that is rooted in the deep, enduring bond of true friendship.

Chapter 6: Trusting God's Timing

Theological Reflection: Explore the concept of trusting in God's perfect timing for love. Ecclesiastes 3:11 can serve as the anchor verse, focusing on the beauty of things happening at the right time.

Introduction: The Divine Clockwork

IN OUR FAST-PACED, instant-gratification culture, waiting can be one of the most challenging aspects of life. This is especially true when it comes to matters of the heart. Whether it's waiting for the right person to come along, waiting for a relationship to develop, or waiting for the right time to take the next step, the process of waiting can feel excruciating. Yet, the Bible assures us that God's timing is perfect, and that His plans are always good. Ecclesiastes 3:11 captures this beautifully: *"He has made everything beautiful in its time. Also, He has put eternity into man's heart, yet so that he cannot find out what God has done from the beginning to the end."*

This verse reminds us that there is a divine timing to all things—a timing that is often beyond our understanding, but always perfect in its execution. Trusting in God's timing, especially in the context of love, requires faith, patience, and a deep reliance on God's sovereignty. It involves surrendering our own desires and timelines, and placing our trust in the One who knows the beginning from the end.

In this chapter, we will explore the concept of trusting in God's perfect timing for love. We will delve into the biblical understanding of God's timing, the challenges of waiting, and the beauty that comes from things happening at the right time. Using Ecclesiastes 3:11 as our anchor verse, we will reflect on how trusting God's timing can lead to a deeper, more fulfilling love—a love that is worth waiting for.

The Biblical Understanding of God's Timing

THROUGHOUT THE BIBLE, we see numerous examples of God's perfect timing at work. From the creation of the world to the birth of Jesus, from the deliverance of the Israelites to the spread of the Gospel, God's timing is evident in every event. The Bible presents time as something that is under God's control, something that He orchestrates according to His divine plan.

In Genesis, the creation account shows God's deliberate and orderly approach to time. Over the course of six days, God created the heavens and the earth, with each day building upon the previous one. This sequence emphasizes that God's work is not random or haphazard; it is purposeful and perfectly timed. Each element of creation came into being at the right moment, according to God's plan.

The story of Abraham and Sarah is another powerful example of God's timing. In Genesis 12, God promises Abraham that he will be the father of a great nation. However, it wasn't until many years later that this promise was fulfilled with the birth of Isaac. During this time of waiting, Abraham and Sarah experienced doubt, frustration, and even moments of taking matters into their own hands, as seen in the birth of Ishmael through Hagar. Yet, when Isaac was finally born, it was clear that God's timing was perfect. Isaac's birth was not just the fulfillment of a promise; it was a testament to God's faithfulness and His ability to make all things beautiful in their time.

The New Testament continues to highlight the importance of God's timing. Galatians 4:4 speaks of the timing of Jesus' birth: *"But when the fullness of time had come, God sent forth his Son, born of woman, born under the law."* The phrase "the fullness of time" indicates that Jesus' arrival on earth was not random; it was perfectly timed according to God's plan. The world was ready for the coming of the Messiah, and Jesus' birth, life, death, and resurrection unfolded precisely as God had intended.

Similarly, the spread of the Gospel in the early church was guided by God's timing. Acts 1:7 records Jesus telling His disciples, *"It is not for you to know times or seasons that the Father has fixed by his own authority."* This verse underscores the truth that God's timing is sovereign, and that we, as His followers, are called to trust in His timing even when we do not fully understand it.

The Challenges of Waiting

DESPITE THE BIBLICAL assurance of God's perfect timing, waiting can be incredibly difficult, especially in the context of love. The desire for companionship, marriage, or a deeper connection with someone can make the waiting period feel long and lonely. In these moments, it is easy to question God's timing, to wonder why things aren't happening according to our plans, or to feel frustrated by the lack of progress.

One of the primary challenges of waiting is the temptation to take matters into our own hands. When we feel that God is moving too slowly, we may be tempted to rush into a relationship that is not right for us, to compromise our values, or to settle for less than God's best. This temptation is evident in the story of Abraham and Sarah, who, in their impatience, decided to have a child through Hagar. While this decision brought temporary relief, it ultimately led to complications and heartache, as it was not part of God's perfect plan.

Another challenge of waiting is dealing with the uncertainty and ambiguity of the future. Unlike God, who knows the end from the beginning, we are limited in our understanding of the future. This can create anxiety and fear, as we wonder if we will ever find the love we are seeking or if our dreams will ever be fulfilled. This uncertainty can be especially challenging in a culture that values immediate results and instant gratification.

The waiting period can also be marked by feelings of loneliness and isolation. Watching others enter into relationships, get married, or start families can intensify the sense of being left behind. In these moments, it is easy to feel forgotten or overlooked by God, leading to doubt and discouragement.

However, while the challenges of waiting are real, they also present an opportunity for growth and deepening faith. Waiting on God's timing teaches us patience, trust, and dependence on Him. It helps us to develop a deeper relationship with God, as we learn to rely on His strength and guidance rather than our own understanding.

Ecclesiastes 3:11: The Beauty of God's Timing

ECCLESIASTES 3:11 OFFERS a profound truth about the nature of God's timing: *"He has made everything beautiful in its time. Also, He has put eternity into man's heart, yet so that he cannot find out what God has done from the beginning to the end."* This verse highlights two key aspects of God's timing: its beauty and its mystery.

The Beauty of God's Timing: The phrase "He has made everything beautiful in its time" speaks to the perfection of God's timing. When things happen according to God's plan, they unfold in a way that is both harmonious and beautiful. This beauty is not just about the outward appearance of events; it is about the rightness and fittingness of God's actions.

In the context of love, this means that when a relationship comes together according to God's timing, it is marked by a sense of peace, joy, and fulfillment. The relationship unfolds naturally and organically, without the need for force or manipulation. Both partners feel a deep sense of alignment with God's will, and the relationship is characterized by mutual respect, love, and commitment.

Moreover, the beauty of God's timing is often evident in the way He prepares us for the relationship. During the waiting period, God is at work in our hearts, shaping our character, deepening our faith, and aligning our desires with His will. When the right person comes along at the right time, we are better equipped to love and serve them in a way that honors God. The relationship becomes a reflection of God's love and grace, and it brings glory to Him.

The Mystery of God's Timing: The second part of Ecclesiastes 3:11—"He has put eternity into man's heart, yet so that he cannot find out what God has done from the beginning to the end"—speaks to the mystery of God's timing. While we have a sense of the eternal and a longing for things to be made right, we are limited in our understanding of how God is working out His plan.

This mystery can be both comforting and challenging. On the one hand, it reminds us that God's ways are higher than our ways and that His understanding is far beyond our own. On the other hand, it requires us to trust God even when we cannot see the full picture or understand why things are happening the way they are.

In the context of love, this means that we may not always understand why we are still waiting, why certain relationships did not work out, or why the timing seems off. However, trusting in the mystery of God's timing means surrendering our need for control and embracing the uncertainty with faith. It means believing that God is at work, even when we cannot see it, and that His timing is always perfect, even when it does not align with our expectations.

Trusting God's Timing in Love

TRUSTING GOD'S TIMING in love is not a passive act; it requires active faith, patience, and a willingness to surrender our desires to God. It involves recognizing that God's timing is not just about when things happen but also about how they happen and who we become in the process.

1. Surrendering Our Timelines: One of the first steps in trusting God's timing is surrendering our own timelines and expectations. This can be challenging, especially if we have specific plans or desires for when certain events should occur, such as getting married or starting a family. However, surrendering our timelines means acknowledging that God's plan is better than our own and that His timing is perfect.

This surrender is not about giving up on our dreams or desires; it is about entrusting them to God and allowing Him to bring them to fruition in His time. Proverbs 16:9 reminds us, *"The heart of man plans his way, but the Lord establishes his steps."* When we surrender our plans to God, we open ourselves to the possibility that His timing may be different from our own, but it is always for our good.

2. Cultivating Patience: Patience is a key aspect of trusting God's timing. The waiting period can be difficult, but it is also an opportunity to develop patience and perseverance. James 1:3-4 encourages us to embrace patience as a means of spiritual growth: *"For you know that the testing of your faith produces steadfastness. And let steadfastness have its full effect, that you may be

perfect and complete, lacking in nothing."* Patience allows us to trust in God's timing without becoming anxious or frustrated. It helps us to remain faithful and hopeful, even when the waiting period is longer than we anticipated.

Cultivating patience involves staying focused on God's promises and trusting that He is at work, even when we cannot see immediate results. It also involves being present in the moment, rather than constantly looking to the future. By embracing the present, we can fully experience the blessings and opportunities that God has placed before us, even as we wait for the fulfillment of our desires.

3. Embracing the Process: Trusting God's timing also means embracing the process of growth and preparation that occurs during the waiting period. God often uses this time to shape our character, deepen our faith, and align our desires with His will. Rather than viewing the waiting period as a time of inactivity or delay, we can see it as a time of preparation for the blessings that God has in store for us.

Isaiah 40:31 offers a beautiful promise for those who wait on the Lord: *"But they who wait for the Lord shall renew their strength; they shall mount up with wings like eagles; they shall run and not be weary; they shall walk and not faint."* This verse reminds us that waiting on God is not passive; it is an active process of renewal and growth. As we wait, God strengthens us, equips us, and prepares us for the journey ahead.

4. Trusting in God's Goodness: At the heart of trusting God's timing is a deep belief in His goodness. Romans 8:28 assures us that *"And we know that in all things God works for the good of those who love him, who have been called according to his purpose."* This promise is a reminder that God is always working for our good, even when we do not understand His timing or His methods.

Trusting in God's goodness means believing that His plans are always for our benefit, even when they do not align with our own desires or expectations. It means trusting that God knows what is best for us and that He will bring about His purposes in our lives in His perfect time.

The Fruit of Trusting God's Timing

WHEN WE TRUST IN GOD'S timing, we experience a deep sense of peace and contentment, knowing that our lives are in His hands. This trust also bears fruit in our relationships, as it allows us to enter into love with a sense of security and confidence, knowing that God has orchestrated the relationship according to His plan.

1. Peace and Contentment: One of the most immediate fruits of trusting God's timing is the peace that comes from knowing that we are not in control but that we are in the hands of a loving and sovereign God. Philippians 4:6-7 speaks to this peace: *"Do not be anxious about anything, but in everything by prayer and supplication with thanksgiving let your requests be made known to God. And the peace of God, which surpasses all understanding, will guard your hearts and your minds in Christ Jesus."*

This peace is not dependent on our circumstances; it is a gift from God that transcends our understanding. When we trust in God's timing, we are free from the anxiety and stress that often accompany uncertainty. We can rest in the assurance that God is in control and that He is working all things together for our good.

2. Confidence in Relationships: Trusting God's timing also brings a sense of confidence and security in our relationships. When we believe that God has orchestrated the timing and circumstances of a relationship, we can enter into it with a sense of peace and assurance. We do not need to worry about whether we are making the right decision or whether the timing is right; we can trust that God has already gone before us and prepared the way.

This confidence allows us to be fully present in the relationship, without being consumed by doubts or fears. It also helps us to trust our partner, knowing that God has brought us together according to His plan. This trust fosters a deeper connection and a stronger bond between partners, as it is rooted in a shared faith in God's timing.

3. A Deeper Relationship with God: Trusting God's timing deepens our relationship with Him, as it requires us to rely on His wisdom, guidance, and strength. The process of waiting and trusting helps us to grow in our faith and to develop a closer, more intimate relationship with God. As we surrender our

desires and timelines to Him, we learn to trust Him more fully and to seek His will above our own.

This deepened relationship with God is one of the greatest blessings of trusting in His timing. It transforms our perspective, helps us to see our circumstances through the lens of faith, and draws us closer to the heart of God.

Practical Steps for Trusting God's Timing

TRUSTING GOD'S TIMING is a journey that requires intentionality and commitment. Here are some practical steps to help you cultivate trust in God's timing, especially in the context of love:

1. Pray for Guidance: Begin by bringing your desires and concerns to God in prayer. Ask Him for guidance, wisdom, and the strength to trust in His timing. Prayer is a powerful tool for aligning your heart with God's will and for finding peace in His presence.

2. Surrender Your Timeline: Make a conscious decision to surrender your own timeline and expectations to God. This might involve writing down your plans and desires and then offering them up to God in prayer, asking Him to bring them to fruition in His time.

3. Cultivate Patience: Practice patience by focusing on the present moment and trusting that God is at work, even when you cannot see the immediate results. Patience is developed over time, so be gentle with yourself as you learn to wait on God.

4. Embrace the Process: Recognize that the waiting period is not a time of inactivity but a time of growth and preparation. Embrace the opportunities for personal and spiritual growth that God has placed before you, and trust that He is preparing you for the blessings that are to come.

5. Seek Support: Surround yourself with a community of believers who can support you in your journey of trusting God's timing. Share your struggles and victories with them, and seek their encouragement and prayers.

6. Reflect on God's Faithfulness: Take time to reflect on God's faithfulness in your life. Remember the times when He has come through for you in the past, and let these memories strengthen your faith in His timing for the future.

7. Trust in God's Goodness: Remind yourself daily of God's goodness and His promises. Meditate on Scriptures that speak to His faithfulness, sovereignty, and love, and let these truths anchor your trust in His timing.

Conclusion: The Beauty of Waiting for God's Perfect Time

TRUSTING GOD'S TIMING for love is not always easy, but it is always worth it. Ecclesiastes 3:11 reminds us that God makes everything beautiful in its time. This beauty is not just about the outward appearance of events; it is about the rightness, harmony, and fittingness of God's actions.

As you navigate the journey of seeking and waiting for love, may you be encouraged to trust in God's perfect timing. Surrender your timeline to Him, cultivate patience, and embrace the process of growth and preparation. Trust that God is at work in your life, even when you cannot see the full picture, and believe that His plans are always for your good.

May you experience the peace, confidence, and deepened relationship with God that comes from trusting in His timing. And may you find that the love God has prepared for you is truly worth the wait—a love that is beautiful, fulfilling, and perfectly timed according to His divine plan.

Chapter 7: Overcoming Loneliness with God's Presence

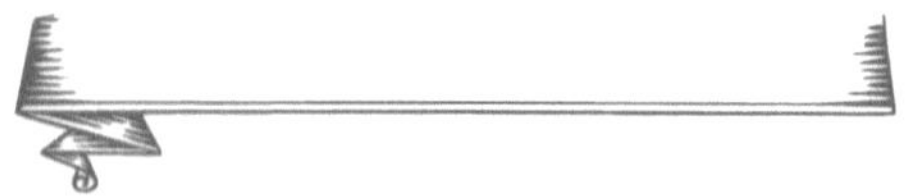

Theological Reflection: Reflect on how God's presence can fill the void of loneliness while waiting for love. Use Psalm 23:4 to emphasize that God's companionship is constant and reassuring.

Introduction: The Ache of Loneliness

LONELINESS IS A POWERFUL and often overwhelming emotion. It can leave a person feeling isolated, unworthy, and forgotten. In the context of waiting for love, loneliness can be especially acute. The longing for companionship, the desire to be known and loved, and the fear of being left alone can create a deep sense of emptiness that seems impossible to fill. Yet, the Bible assures us that even in our loneliest moments, we are never truly alone. God's presence is always with us, offering comfort, strength, and companionship.

Psalm 23:4, one of the most beloved verses in Scripture, speaks directly to this truth: *"Even though I walk through the valley of the shadow of death, I will fear no evil, for you are with me; your rod and your staff, they comfort me."* This verse reminds us that God's presence is constant and reassuring, even in the darkest and most difficult times. It is this presence that has the power to fill the void of loneliness and to provide the companionship we seek.

In this chapter, we will explore how God's presence can help us overcome loneliness, particularly in the context of waiting for love. We will reflect on the nature of loneliness, the promises of God's companionship, and practical ways to cultivate an awareness of His presence in our daily lives. Using Psalm 23:4 as our anchor, we will delve into the deep and abiding comfort that comes from knowing that God is always with us, even when we feel most alone.

The Nature of Loneliness

LONELINESS IS A COMPLEX and multifaceted emotion that can be experienced in different ways. It is important to recognize that loneliness is not simply about being physically alone; it is about feeling disconnected from others, from oneself, and even from God. This disconnection can lead to a profound sense of isolation and emptiness, which can be difficult to overcome.

1. Emotional Loneliness: Emotional loneliness occurs when we feel that we lack close, meaningful relationships. This type of loneliness is often experienced when we desire deeper emotional connections with others but feel that those connections are missing or inadequate. In the context of waiting for love, emotional loneliness can be particularly painful, as it is often tied to the desire for a romantic partner with whom to share life's joys and challenges.

2. Social Loneliness: Social loneliness arises when we feel that we do not belong to a community or social group. This can occur when we are physically separated from others, such as during a move to a new city, or when we feel that we do not fit in with the people around us. Social loneliness can also be experienced in the context of waiting for love, especially when we see others around us entering into relationships, getting married, or starting families.

3. Existential Loneliness: Existential loneliness is a deeper form of loneliness that stems from a sense of disconnection from one's purpose, identity, and meaning in life. This type of loneliness can lead to feelings of despair, hopelessness, and a sense of being adrift in the world. Existential loneliness often accompanies periods of waiting, as we question our purpose and wonder why certain aspects of our lives have not yet fallen into place.

While loneliness is a natural and common human experience, it can be exacerbated by the pressures and expectations of our culture. In a society that often equates success with romantic relationships, marriage, and family, those who are single or waiting for love can feel marginalized or left behind. This can lead to a sense of inadequacy and worthlessness, further intensifying the feelings of loneliness.

However, it is important to remember that loneliness, though painful, is not an indication of failure or unworthiness. It is a part of the human experience, one that can be transformed and redeemed through a deeper relationship with God. When we bring our loneliness to God, we open ourselves to the healing and comfort that only His presence can provide.

The Promise of God's Presence

THE BIBLE IS FILLED with promises of God's presence, offering reassurance that we are never truly alone, no matter how we may feel. From the Old Testament to the New Testament, God continually affirms His commitment to be with His people, providing comfort, guidance, and companionship.

1. God's Presence in the Old Testament: In the Old Testament, God's presence is often depicted as a source of strength and protection for His people. In Deuteronomy 31:6, Moses encourages the Israelites as they prepare to enter the Promised Land: *"Be strong and courageous. Do not be afraid or terrified because of them, for the Lord your God goes with you; he will never leave you nor forsake you."* This promise of God's unwavering presence is a source of courage and reassurance for the Israelites as they face an uncertain future.

Similarly, in Joshua 1:9, God speaks directly to Joshua, reaffirming His presence as Joshua takes on the mantle of leadership: *"Have I not commanded you? Be strong and courageous. Do not be frightened, and do not be dismayed, for the Lord your God is with you wherever you go."* This verse underscores the constancy of God's presence, offering Joshua the confidence to lead the people with faith and trust in God's guidance.

The Psalms, too, are replete with references to God's presence as a source of comfort and refuge. Psalm 46:1 declares, *"God is our refuge and strength, an ever-present help in trouble."* This verse speaks to the accessibility of God's presence, emphasizing that He is always near and ready to provide help in times of need.

2. God's Presence in the New Testament: In the New Testament, the promise of God's presence takes on a new dimension with the coming of Jesus Christ, who is called *"Emmanuel,"* meaning *"God with us"* (Matthew 1:23). Jesus' life, death, and resurrection are the ultimate fulfillment of God's promise to be with His people, bridging the gap between humanity and the divine.

Throughout His ministry, Jesus emphasizes the importance of God's presence in the lives of His followers. In John 14:16-17, Jesus promises the Holy Spirit, who will dwell with and within believers: *"And I will ask the Father, and he will give you another Helper, to be with you forever, even the Spirit of truth, whom the world cannot receive, because it neither sees him nor knows him. You know him, for he dwells with you and will be in you."* The Holy Spirit, as the indwelling presence of God, provides believers with constant companionship, guidance, and comfort.

Moreover, Jesus reassures His disciples of His continued presence even after His ascension. In Matthew 28:20, He promises, *"And behold, I am with you always, to the end of the age."* This promise is a source of comfort and strength for believers, affirming that Jesus' presence is not limited by time or space but is a constant reality in the lives of those who follow Him.

3. The Assurance of Psalm 23:4: Psalm 23:4, one of the most comforting verses in the Bible, encapsulates the promise of God's presence in a powerful way: *"Even though I walk through the valley of the shadow of death, I will fear no evil, for you are with me; your rod and your staff, they comfort me."* This verse speaks to the reality of God's presence even in the darkest and most challenging moments of life.

The imagery of the valley of the shadow of death evokes a sense of danger, uncertainty, and fear. Yet, the psalmist declares that even in this valley, he will not be afraid, because God is with him. The mention of the rod and staff, tools used by shepherds to guide and protect their sheep, further emphasizes God's role as a protector and guide. These symbols of God's presence offer comfort and reassurance, reminding us that we are not alone, even when we walk through the darkest valleys.

In the context of loneliness, Psalm 23:4 serves as a powerful reminder that God's presence is constant and reassuring. Whether we are facing the loneliness of waiting for love, the loneliness of loss, or the loneliness of feeling misunderstood, we can take comfort in the knowledge that God is with us, guiding and protecting us every step of the way.

Overcoming Loneliness with God's Presence

WHILE THE PROMISES of God's presence offer comfort and reassurance, the challenge lies in experiencing and embracing that presence in the midst of loneliness. Overcoming loneliness with God's presence requires intentionality and a willingness to seek Him in the quiet, often painful, moments of life.

1. Cultivating Awareness of God's Presence: The first step in overcoming loneliness with God's presence is to cultivate an awareness of His presence in our daily lives. This involves shifting our focus from our feelings of loneliness to the reality of God's constant companionship.

One way to cultivate this awareness is through prayer and meditation. Psalm 46:10 encourages us to *"Be still, and know that I am God."* Taking time to be still in God's presence, to meditate on His Word, and to listen for His voice can help us become more attuned to His presence. This stillness allows us to quiet the noise of our anxieties and fears, and to focus on the truth that God is with us, even in our loneliness.

Another way to cultivate awareness of God's presence is through the practice of gratitude. Philippians 4:6-7 reminds us, *"Do not be anxious about anything, but in everything by prayer and supplication with thanksgiving let your requests be made known to God. And the peace of God, which surpasses all understanding, will guard your hearts and your minds in Christ Jesus."* By focusing on the blessings and gifts that God has already provided, we can shift our perspective from what we lack to what we have, thereby deepening our awareness of God's presence in our lives.

2. Embracing God's Companionship: To overcome loneliness, we must also learn to embrace God's companionship. This means recognizing that God is not just a distant deity but a personal, loving companion who desires to walk with us through every aspect of our lives.

One way to embrace God's companionship is by inviting Him into the ordinary moments of our day. Whether we are going for a walk, cooking a meal, or simply sitting quietly, we can turn these moments into opportunities to connect with God. By talking to Him, sharing our thoughts and feelings, and asking for His guidance, we can experience His presence in a tangible way.

Another way to embrace God's companionship is by remembering that He is our Shepherd, as depicted in Psalm 23. A shepherd's role is to care for, protect, and guide the sheep, and this is precisely what God does for us. When we embrace God as our Shepherd, we can trust that He is leading us, even when we feel lost or alone. This trust allows us to rest in His care, knowing that He is with us and that He will never leave us.

3. Finding Comfort in God's Promises: The promises of God's presence are a source of comfort and strength, especially in times of loneliness. To overcome loneliness, we must hold fast to these promises and allow them to shape our perspective and our emotions.

Isaiah 41:10 offers one such promise: *"Fear not, for I am with you; be not dismayed, for I am your God; I will strengthen you, I will help you, I will uphold you with my righteous right hand."* This verse reassures us that God is not only with us but that He is actively working to strengthen and uphold us. When we feel overwhelmed by loneliness, we can find comfort in the knowledge that God is our source of strength and support.

Similarly, Deuteronomy 31:8 promises, *"It is the Lord who goes before you. He will be with you; he will not leave you or forsake you. Do not fear or be dismayed."* This promise reminds us that God is not only with us in the present but that He goes before us, preparing the way and ensuring that we are never alone.

By meditating on these promises and allowing them to take root in our hearts, we can find comfort and reassurance in the midst of loneliness. These promises serve as a reminder that God's presence is constant, even when our circumstances are challenging.

4. Connecting with Others Through God's Love: While God's presence is the ultimate source of companionship, it is also important to recognize that God often works through others to provide comfort and support. Connecting with others through God's love can help alleviate loneliness and provide a sense of community and belonging.

Hebrews 10:24-25 encourages believers to support one another: *"And let us consider how to stir up one another to love and good works, not neglecting to meet together, as is the habit of some, but encouraging one another, and all the more as you see the Day drawing near."* By seeking out and nurturing relationships with fellow believers, we can experience the love and support of God's family.

Additionally, reaching out to others who may be experiencing loneliness can be a powerful way to combat our own feelings of isolation. When we serve and care for others, we not only reflect God's love but also build meaningful connections that can help to alleviate loneliness.

5. Trusting in God's Plan: Overcoming loneliness with God's presence also involves trusting in His plan for our lives. This means believing that God has a purpose for our season of waiting and that He is using it to shape us, grow us, and prepare us for the future.

Jeremiah 29:11 offers a powerful reminder of God's plans: *"For I know the plans I have for you, declares the Lord, plans for welfare and not for evil, to give you a future and a hope."* This verse reassures us that God's plans are good and that He is working all things together for our benefit. When we trust in God's plan, we can find peace in the waiting, knowing that He is with us and that He is guiding us toward a hopeful future.

Practical Steps for Embracing God's Presence

EMBRACING GOD'S PRESENCE in the midst of loneliness is a journey that requires intentionality and commitment. Here are some practical steps to help you cultivate a deeper awareness of God's presence and overcome loneliness:

1. Create a Sacred Space: Designate a specific place in your home where you can spend time with God. This could be a corner of a room, a comfortable chair, or even a spot in your garden. Use this space for prayer, meditation, and reflection, and make it a place where you can connect with God and experience His presence.

2. Practice Daily Devotion: Set aside time each day to read Scripture, pray, and meditate on God's promises. Daily devotion helps to anchor your day in God's presence and provides a consistent reminder of His companionship.

3. Engage in Worship: Worship is a powerful way to experience God's presence. Whether through music, singing, or simply expressing your gratitude to God, worship helps to shift your focus from your loneliness to the greatness and goodness of God.

4. Journal Your Thoughts and Prayers: Keeping a journal can be a helpful way to process your emotions and to document your journey of overcoming

loneliness. Write down your thoughts, prayers, and reflections, and use your journal as a way to communicate with God and to track His faithfulness in your life.

5. Connect with a Community: Seek out a community of believers who can support you in your journey. This could be a church group, a Bible study, or a fellowship group. Connecting with others who share your faith can provide encouragement, support, and a sense of belonging.

6. Serve Others: Look for opportunities to serve others who may also be experiencing loneliness. Volunteering, reaching out to a friend, or offering a listening ear can help to shift your focus from your own loneliness to the needs of others. Serving others not only reflects God's love but also helps to build meaningful connections.

7. Rest in God's Promises: Take time to meditate on the promises of God's presence in Scripture. Write down verses that speak to you, memorize them, and reflect on them throughout your day. Allow these promises to fill your heart with peace and reassurance.

Conclusion: The Comfort of God's Constant Presence

LONELINESS IS A REALITY that many of us face, especially in the context of waiting for love. However, the Bible assures us that even in our loneliest moments, we are never truly alone. God's presence is constant and reassuring, offering comfort, strength, and companionship that can fill the void of loneliness.

Psalm 23:4 reminds us that even as we walk through the darkest valleys, we need not fear, for God is with us. His rod and staff comfort us, guiding and protecting us every step of the way. This promise of God's presence is a source of profound comfort and reassurance, providing the strength we need to overcome loneliness.

As you navigate the challenges of loneliness, may you be encouraged to seek and embrace God's presence in your life. Cultivate an awareness of His companionship, trust in His promises, and find comfort in the knowledge that He is always with you. Whether through prayer, worship, community, or service, take practical steps to deepen your relationship with God and to experience the fullness of His presence.

In the presence of God, loneliness loses its power. His companionship fills the empty spaces in our hearts, and His love surrounds us, providing the comfort and reassurance we need. May you find peace, hope, and joy in the constant and unchanging presence of God, knowing that He is with you always, even in the moments of deepest loneliness.

Chapter 8: The Significance of Commitment

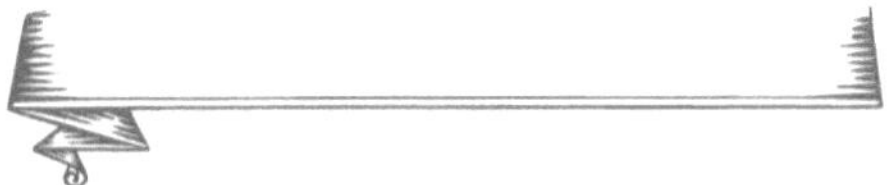

Theological Reflection: Discuss the importance of commitment in love and how waiting is a form of commitment to God's best for us. Reference Ruth 1:16-17, highlighting Ruth's unwavering commitment as an example.

Introduction: The Foundation of Commitment

COMMITMENT IS ONE OF the most powerful and essential elements in any meaningful relationship. Whether in friendships, family ties, or romantic partnerships, commitment serves as the bedrock upon which trust, love, and mutual respect are built. Without commitment, relationships are fragile, subject to the whims of changing emotions and external circumstances. Commitment, however, provides stability, security, and a deep sense of purpose, enabling relationships to endure through challenges and to flourish over time.

In the context of romantic love, commitment takes on a particularly significant role. It is the glue that holds a relationship together, especially when faced with difficulties, misunderstandings, or the inevitable ebb and flow of emotions. Commitment is not merely a promise to stay together; it is a deliberate, ongoing decision to invest in the relationship, to prioritize the well-being of the other person, and to honor the covenant of love.

But commitment is not only crucial in our human relationships; it is also central to our relationship with God. In many ways, waiting for love is itself an act of commitment—an expression of our trust in God's timing and our willingness to seek His best for our lives. This kind of commitment requires patience, faith, and a deep reliance on God's wisdom and goodness.

One of the most poignant examples of commitment in the Bible is found in the story of Ruth. Ruth's unwavering commitment to her mother-in-law, Naomi, and to the God of Israel serves as a powerful illustration of the kind of love and dedication that God calls us to in our relationships. In Ruth 1:16-17, Ruth makes a profound declaration of commitment: *"But Ruth said, 'Do not urge me to leave you or to return from following you. For where you go I will go, and where you lodge I will lodge. Your people shall be my people, and your God my God. Where you die I will die, and there will I be buried. May the Lord do so to me and more also if anything but death parts me from you.'"*

In this chapter, we will explore the significance of commitment in love, drawing from Ruth's example to understand how waiting for love can be an expression of our commitment to God's best for us. We will reflect on the nature of commitment, the challenges and rewards of remaining committed, and the ways in which commitment shapes and deepens our relationships.

The Nature of Commitment

COMMITMENT IS OFTEN misunderstood in our contemporary culture, where it is sometimes seen as restrictive or burdensome. However, true commitment is not about being trapped or limited; rather, it is about making a conscious choice to invest in something or someone that we value deeply. Commitment is rooted in love, and it is expressed through our actions, decisions, and attitudes.

1. Commitment as a Covenant: In the Bible, commitment is often depicted as a covenant—a solemn and binding agreement between two parties. A covenant is more than just a contract; it is a sacred promise that involves the whole person, including their heart, mind, and soul. In a covenant relationship, both parties commit to honoring the agreement, even when it is difficult or costly.

The most significant example of a covenant in the Bible is the covenant between God and His people. Throughout Scripture, God repeatedly enters into covenants with His people, promising to be their God and to bless them, while also calling them to be faithful to Him. These covenants are marked by steadfast love, faithfulness, and a deep sense of commitment.

In the context of romantic love, commitment can be understood as a form of covenant—a promise to love, honor, and cherish the other person, regardless of the circumstances. This kind of commitment goes beyond mere feelings or attraction; it is a deliberate choice to prioritize the relationship and to invest in its growth and flourishing.

2. Commitment as a Choice: Commitment is also a choice—one that we must make repeatedly throughout our lives. It is not a one-time decision, but an ongoing process of choosing to stay true to our promises, even when it is difficult or inconvenient. This choice is often tested in the face of challenges, such as misunderstandings, disagreements, or external pressures.

In a romantic relationship, the choice to remain committed can be challenging, especially when emotions fluctuate or when the relationship encounters difficulties. However, it is precisely in these moments that commitment becomes most meaningful. By choosing to stay committed, we demonstrate our love and respect for the other person, and we create a foundation of trust that can withstand the trials of life.

3. Commitment as Sacrifice: True commitment often involves sacrifice. This may mean giving up certain personal desires, comforts, or conveniences for the sake of the relationship. It may also involve putting the needs of the other person above our own, or making difficult decisions that require courage and faith.

In the Bible, the ultimate example of sacrificial commitment is Jesus Christ, who willingly laid down His life for the sake of humanity. In Philippians 2:5-8, we read about the self-emptying love of Christ: *"Have this mind among yourselves, which is yours in Christ Jesus, who, though he was in the form of God, did not count equality with God a thing to be grasped, but emptied himself, by taking the form of a servant, being born in the likeness of men. And being found in human form, he humbled himself by becoming obedient to the point of death, even death on a cross."* Jesus' commitment to His mission and to humanity is the ultimate model of sacrificial love.

In our relationships, we are called to emulate this kind of commitment—one that is willing to sacrifice for the good of the other person and for the sake of the relationship. This sacrificial commitment is not about losing ourselves; rather, it is about finding a deeper and more meaningful connection through love and self-giving.

Ruth's Unwavering Commitment: A Biblical Example

THE STORY OF RUTH IS one of the most beautiful and inspiring examples of commitment in the Bible. Ruth's unwavering dedication to her mother-in-law, Naomi, and to the God of Israel, offers profound insights into the nature of commitment and its transformative power.

1. The Context of Ruth's Commitment: Ruth's story begins with tragedy. After the death of her husband and her two sons, Naomi, a widow from Bethlehem, finds herself alone in a foreign land, Moab. She decides to return to Bethlehem, urging her two daughters-in-law, Ruth and Orpah, to return to their own families. While Orpah reluctantly agrees, Ruth refuses to leave Naomi, declaring her famous words of commitment in Ruth 1:16-17.

Ruth's decision to stay with Naomi is remarkable for several reasons. First, Ruth is a Moabite, a member of a people who were often viewed with suspicion and hostility by the Israelites. By choosing to accompany Naomi to Bethlehem, Ruth is leaving behind her homeland, her family, and her culture, to live as a foreigner in a land where she may not be welcomed.

Second, Ruth is making this decision with no guarantee of security or provision. Naomi is an elderly widow with no means of support, and Ruth herself is a widow with no children. The future is uncertain and fraught with potential hardship, yet Ruth chooses to stay with Naomi out of love and loyalty.

2. The Depth of Ruth's Commitment: Ruth's commitment is not just to Naomi, but also to the God of Israel. In her declaration, she says, *"Your people shall be my people, and your God my God."* This is a significant statement, as it indicates Ruth's willingness to adopt Naomi's faith and to embrace the God of Israel as her own. This commitment is not merely cultural or familial; it is spiritual and deeply personal.

Ruth's commitment to Naomi and to God is total and unwavering. She is willing to sacrifice her own comfort, security, and future for the sake of her relationship with Naomi and her faith in God. This kind of commitment is rare and extraordinary, and it demonstrates the power of love and loyalty to transcend personal desires and circumstances.

3. The Reward of Ruth's Commitment: Ruth's commitment is ultimately rewarded by God. After arriving in Bethlehem, Ruth works tirelessly to provide for Naomi, gleaning in the fields to gather food. Her hard work and faithfulness catch the attention of Boaz, a wealthy and respected man in Bethlehem. Boaz is moved by Ruth's dedication to Naomi and her humility, and he eventually marries her, securing both her and Naomi's future.

Ruth's story culminates in a beautiful reversal of fortune. From a position of vulnerability and uncertainty, Ruth becomes the wife of Boaz and the great-grandmother of King David. Her commitment not only changes her own life but also plays a crucial role in the lineage of Jesus Christ, the Messiah.

Ruth's story teaches us that commitment, when rooted in love and faithfulness, can lead to unexpected blessings and opportunities. Her unwavering dedication to Naomi and to God serves as a powerful example of how commitment can transform our lives and bring about God's best for us.

Commitment in Romantic Relationships

THE SIGNIFICANCE OF commitment in romantic relationships cannot be overstated. In a culture that often prioritizes personal fulfillment and individualism, the idea of commitment can sometimes be seen as limiting or even outdated. However, true commitment is essential for the health and longevity of any romantic relationship. It is the foundation upon which trust, intimacy, and love are built, and it is what enables a relationship to grow and deepen over time.

1. Commitment as the Foundation of Trust: Trust is a vital component of any romantic relationship, and it is built on the foundation of commitment. When both partners are committed to the relationship, they create an environment of safety and security, where trust can flourish. This trust allows both partners to be vulnerable with one another, to share their deepest thoughts and feelings, and to rely on one another for support.

Commitment also provides the assurance that both partners are in the relationship for the long haul, which fosters a sense of stability and confidence.

This stability is especially important in times of conflict or difficulty, as it allows both partners to work through challenges without fear of abandonment or betrayal.

2. Commitment and Emotional Intimacy: Emotional intimacy is another crucial aspect of a healthy romantic relationship, and it is closely tied to commitment. Emotional intimacy involves sharing one's inner world with another person—one's thoughts, feelings, dreams, and fears. This level of intimacy requires a deep sense of trust and security, which can only be achieved through commitment.

When both partners are committed to the relationship, they are willing to invest the time and effort needed to develop emotional intimacy. They are also more likely to prioritize the relationship, making it a safe space for vulnerability and connection. This emotional intimacy, in turn, deepens the bond between the partners and strengthens the relationship.

3. Commitment and Conflict Resolution: Every relationship will face conflicts and challenges, but commitment is what enables couples to navigate these difficulties successfully. When both partners are committed to the relationship, they are more likely to approach conflicts with a mindset of collaboration rather than competition. Instead of trying to "win" the argument or prove the other person wrong, they focus on finding a solution that benefits the relationship as a whole.

Commitment also means being willing to make sacrifices and compromises for the sake of the relationship. This may involve setting aside personal preferences, apologizing when necessary, or making changes to one's behavior. By remaining committed to the relationship, both partners demonstrate their willingness to put the relationship first, even in the face of challenges.

4. Commitment and Longevity: Finally, commitment is essential for the longevity of a romantic relationship. While emotions and attractions may fluctuate over time, commitment provides the stability needed to weather the ups and downs of life. It is the glue that holds the relationship together, even when circumstances are difficult or when the initial excitement has faded.

Research has shown that commitment is one of the most important predictors of relationship satisfaction and longevity. Couples who are committed to their relationship are more likely to stay together and to experience higher levels of happiness and fulfillment. This is because commitment fosters a sense of security, trust, and mutual respect, which are essential for a healthy and lasting relationship.

Waiting as a Form of Commitment

WAITING FOR LOVE CAN be one of the most challenging aspects of life, especially in a culture that often equates success with being in a relationship. However, waiting can also be a powerful expression of commitment—both to God and to the belief that His timing and plans are better than our own.

1. Commitment to God's Best: Waiting for love is a form of commitment to God's best for our lives. It involves trusting that God has a plan for us and that His timing is perfect, even when it does not align with our own desires or expectations. This kind of commitment requires faith and patience, as we surrender our timelines and preferences to God and trust that He knows what is best for us.

In Psalm 37:7, we are encouraged to *"Be still before the Lord and wait patiently for him; do not fret when people succeed in their ways, when they carry out their wicked schemes."* This verse reminds us that waiting on God is not passive; it is an active expression of trust and commitment. By waiting for God's best, we demonstrate our belief that His plans are good and that He is working all things together for our benefit.

2. Cultivating Patience and Faith: Waiting for love also cultivates patience and faith—two essential qualities for any committed relationship. Patience allows us to endure the waiting period without becoming anxious or discouraged, while faith helps us to trust that God is at work, even when we cannot see the immediate results.

James 1:4 encourages us to let patience have its full effect: *"Let perseverance finish its work so that you may be mature and complete, not lacking anything."* This verse speaks to the transformative power of patience, which shapes our character and prepares us for the blessings that God has in store for us. By waiting patiently for love, we allow God to work in our hearts, shaping us into the people He has called us to be.

3. Commitment to Personal Growth: The waiting period is also an opportunity for personal growth and self-reflection. During this time, we can focus on developing our relationship with God, cultivating our gifts and talents, and becoming the best version of ourselves. This commitment to personal growth not only benefits us individually but also prepares us for a future relationship, where we can bring our whole selves to the partnership.

Proverbs 16:3 encourages us to commit our work to the Lord: *"Commit to the Lord whatever you do, and he will establish your plans."* By committing our time and efforts to personal growth during the waiting period, we align ourselves with God's purposes and allow Him to establish our plans according to His will.

4. Trusting in God's Timing: Finally, waiting for love is an expression of our trust in God's timing. Ecclesiastes 3:11 reminds us that *"He has made everything beautiful in its time."* This verse speaks to the perfection of God's timing, which often differs from our own but is always good.

Trusting in God's timing means surrendering our impatience and anxiety to Him, and believing that He will bring the right person into our lives at the right time. It also means being open to the possibility that God's plans for us may look different from what we expected, but that they are ultimately for our good.

The Rewards of Commitment

WHILE COMMITMENT REQUIRES effort, sacrifice, and patience, it also brings with it profound rewards—both in our relationships with others and in our relationship with God. These rewards include a deep sense of fulfillment, joy, and peace, as well as the assurance that we are living in alignment with God's will.

1. The Reward of Deepened Relationships: One of the most significant rewards of commitment is the deepening of our relationships. When we remain committed to our relationships, we create an environment of trust, security, and mutual respect. This allows our relationships to grow and flourish, leading to greater intimacy, connection, and love.

In romantic relationships, commitment fosters a sense of unity and partnership, where both partners are working together toward a common goal.

This unity strengthens the relationship and helps it to withstand the challenges and trials of life. As a result, committed relationships are often more fulfilling, satisfying, and long-lasting.

2. The Reward of Personal Growth: Commitment also leads to personal growth and transformation. When we remain committed to our goals, our values, and our relationships, we develop qualities such as patience, perseverance, and self-discipline. These qualities not only benefit us in our personal lives but also enhance our relationships with others.

In the context of waiting for love, the commitment to personal growth during the waiting period can lead to greater self-awareness, confidence, and maturity. This growth prepares us for future relationships, where we can bring our best selves to the partnership and contribute to a healthy and thriving relationship.

3. The Reward of God's Blessings: Finally, commitment brings with it the reward of God's blessings. When we remain committed to God's will and trust in His timing, we open ourselves to the blessings that He has in store for us. These blessings may come in the form of a fulfilling relationship, personal growth, or a deeper sense of peace and contentment.

Psalm 37:5 encourages us to commit our way to the Lord and trust in Him: *"Commit your way to the Lord; trust in him, and he will act."* This verse reminds us that when we commit our lives to God and trust in His plans, He will act on our behalf, bringing about His purposes in our lives.

Ruth's story is a powerful example of the rewards of commitment. Her unwavering commitment to Naomi and to God ultimately led to her becoming part of the lineage of Jesus Christ, the Messiah. Ruth's story teaches us that commitment, when rooted in love and faithfulness, can lead to unexpected blessings and opportunities that far exceed our expectations.

Practical Steps for Cultivating Commitment

CULTIVATING COMMITMENT in our relationships and in our walk with God requires intentionality and effort. Here are some practical steps to help you develop and maintain a strong sense of commitment:

1. Clarify Your Values: Take time to reflect on your core values and beliefs, and how they align with your relationships and goals. Clarifying your values helps you to make decisions that are consistent with your commitments and to stay focused on what truly matters.

2. Set Clear Goals: Establish clear and realistic goals for your relationships, personal growth, and spiritual journey. Setting goals helps you to stay motivated and to measure your progress over time. Make sure your goals are aligned with your values and commitments.

3. Communicate Openly: In your relationships, practice open and honest communication with your partner or loved ones. Clear communication is essential for building trust and maintaining commitment. Be willing to express your needs, listen to others, and work together to find solutions.

4. Practice Patience: Cultivate patience in your relationships and in your waiting period. Remember that commitment is a journey, and that growth takes time. Practice patience with yourself and with others, and trust that God is at work, even when progress seems slow.

5. Embrace Sacrifice: Be willing to make sacrifices for the sake of your commitments. This may involve giving up certain comforts or conveniences, or putting the needs of others above your own. Embracing sacrifice is a key aspect of commitment, and it leads to deeper and more meaningful relationships.

6. Seek Support: Surround yourself with a community of believers who can support you in your journey of commitment. Whether through a church group, a mentor, or a close friend, having a support system helps you to stay accountable and encouraged.

7. Trust in God's Timing: Finally, trust in God's timing for your life. Surrender your timelines and expectations to Him, and believe that He is working all things together for your good. Trusting in God's timing is a powerful expression of commitment, and it leads to peace, contentment, and fulfillment.

Conclusion: The Power and Beauty of Commitment

COMMITMENT IS A POWERFUL and essential element in any meaningful relationship—whether with others or with God. It is the foundation of trust, intimacy, and love, and it enables relationships to grow and flourish over time. Ruth's unwavering commitment to Naomi and to God serves as a powerful example of the kind of love and dedication that God calls us to in our relationships.

In the context of waiting for love, commitment is an expression of our trust in God's timing and our willingness to seek His best for our lives. By remaining committed to God's will, we open ourselves to the blessings and opportunities that He has in store for us. This commitment requires patience, faith, and a deep reliance on God's wisdom and goodness.

As you navigate the journey of love and relationships, may you be encouraged to cultivate and embrace commitment in all its forms. Whether in your relationships with others or in your walk with God, let commitment be the foundation upon which you build your life. And may you experience the profound rewards of commitment—a deep sense of fulfillment, joy, and peace, and the assurance that you are living in alignment with God's will.

Commitment is not just about staying together; it is about choosing to love, honor, and cherish the other person every day. It is about making a covenant with God and with your loved ones, and about trusting that God's plans for you are good. As you commit your way to the Lord, may you find that He is faithful to act on your behalf, bringing about His purposes and His best for your life.

Chapter 9: Love as a Reflection of God's Love

Theological Reflection: Delve into how human love, especially one worth waiting for, mirrors God's love for us. 1 Corinthians 13:4-7 can be used to describe the characteristics of divine love that should be present in romantic relationships.

Introduction: The Divine Nature of Love

LOVE IS ONE OF THE most profound and powerful forces in the human experience. It transcends time, culture, and circumstance, touching the deepest parts of our souls. Throughout history, poets, philosophers, and theologians have sought to understand and articulate the nature of love. Yet, as Christians, we recognize that the ultimate source and model of love is God Himself. Scripture reveals that love is not merely an emotion or a human construct; it is the very essence of God's character. As 1 John 4:8 declares, *"God is love."*

In human relationships, particularly in romantic relationships, love can be a beautiful and powerful reflection of God's love for us. However, for love to truly mirror the divine, it must be rooted in the characteristics of God's love as described in Scripture. In 1 Corinthians 13:4-7, the Apostle Paul provides one of the most detailed and profound descriptions of love, outlining the qualities that define it: *"Love is patient and kind; love does not envy or boast; it is not arrogant or rude. It does not insist on its own way; it is not irritable or resentful; it does not rejoice at wrongdoing, but rejoices with the truth. Love bears all things, believes all things, hopes all things, endures all things."*

This passage, often read at weddings and referenced in discussions of love, is not just an idealistic portrayal of love; it is a reflection of God's love for us and a blueprint for how we are to love others, especially in romantic relationships.

In this chapter, we will explore how human love, particularly the kind of love worth waiting for, mirrors God's love. We will delve into the characteristics of divine love as described in 1 Corinthians 13:4-7 and discuss how these qualities should be present in our romantic relationships, helping us to reflect God's love to one another.

The Source and Foundation of Love

BEFORE WE CAN UNDERSTAND how human love reflects God's love, we must first recognize that God is the ultimate source and foundation of all love. The Bible teaches that love originates from God and that our capacity to love others is a result of His love for us.

1. God as the Source of Love: In 1 John 4:7-8, the Apostle John writes, *"Beloved, let us love one another, for love is from God, and whoever loves has been born of God and knows God. Anyone who does not love does not know God, because God is love."* This passage emphasizes that love is not merely a human emotion or an abstract concept; it is a divine attribute that flows from the very nature of God. Because God is love, all true love originates from Him.

This understanding of God as the source of love has profound implications for our relationships. It means that our ability to love others is directly tied to our relationship with God. When we experience God's love for us, it transforms us and enables us to love others in a way that reflects His character. This is why Jesus commands us in John 13:34-35 to love one another as He has loved us: *"A new commandment I give to you, that you love one another: just as I have loved you, you also are to love one another. By this all people will know that you are my disciples, if you have love for one another."*

2. God's Love as the Foundation of Human Love: Because God is the source of all love, our human expressions of love—especially in romantic relationships—are meant to be a reflection of His love. This means that our love should be characterized by the same qualities that define God's love: patience, kindness, selflessness, humility, forgiveness, and endurance. When our love mirrors these divine attributes, it becomes a powerful testimony of God's love to the world.

However, reflecting God's love in our relationships is not something we can do on our own. It requires the work of the Holy Spirit in our hearts, transforming us and enabling us to love others as God loves us. As we grow in our relationship with God, His love flows through us and into our relationships, shaping the way we love others.

3. The Role of the Holy Spirit: The Holy Spirit plays a crucial role in helping us to reflect God's love in our relationships. In Romans 5:5, Paul writes, *"God's love has been poured into our hearts through the Holy Spirit who has been given to us."* The Holy Spirit is the conduit through which God's love enters our hearts, and it is by the Spirit's power that we are able to love others with the same kind of love that God has for us.

The fruit of the Spirit, as described in Galatians 5:22-23, includes love, joy, peace, patience, kindness, goodness, faithfulness, gentleness, and self-control—all qualities that are essential for healthy and God-honoring relationships. As we yield to the work of the Holy Spirit in our lives, we become more like Christ, and our love for others increasingly reflects the love of God.

The Characteristics of Divine Love in 1 Corinthians 13:4-7

1 CORINTHIANS 13:4-7 is often referred to as the "Love Chapter" because of its detailed description of the characteristics of love. However, these verses are not just a poetic ideal; they are a practical guide for how we are to love others, especially in romantic relationships. Let's explore each of these characteristics and consider how they should be present in our relationships.

1. Love is Patient and Kind: The first two qualities that Paul mentions are patience and kindness. Patience is the ability to endure difficult circumstances or the shortcomings of others without becoming angry or frustrated. Kindness, on the other hand, is the act of showing compassion, generosity, and consideration to others.

In romantic relationships, patience and kindness are essential for maintaining harmony and mutual respect. Patience allows us to give our partner the time and space they need to grow, to make mistakes, and to learn. It helps us to respond with grace rather than anger when conflicts arise, and it enables us to wait for God's timing in our relationship.

Kindness, meanwhile, is expressed through our actions and words. It involves treating our partner with gentleness, understanding, and respect. It means being generous with our time, attention, and resources, and seeking to build up and encourage our partner rather than tearing them down.

2. Love Does Not Envy or Boast: Envy and boasting are two sides of the same coin, both rooted in pride. Envy is the desire to have what someone else has, while boasting is the act of flaunting what we have in order to make others feel inferior.

In a romantic relationship, envy and boasting can be destructive. Envy can lead to resentment, jealousy, and competition between partners, while boasting can create feelings of inadequacy and insecurity. True love, however, is not self-centered or competitive; it is humble and content. When we love someone, we celebrate their successes and blessings without feeling threatened or inferior. We seek to build them up rather than to elevate ourselves.

3. Love is Not Arrogant or Rude: Arrogance and rudeness are expressions of a lack of respect and consideration for others. Arrogance involves thinking too highly of oneself and looking down on others, while rudeness involves disregarding the feelings and needs of others.

In a romantic relationship, arrogance and rudeness can create a toxic environment where one partner feels disrespected and devalued. True love, however, is humble and considerate. It involves treating our partner with dignity and respect, valuing their opinions and feelings, and being mindful of how our words and actions affect them.

4. Love Does Not Insist on Its Own Way: One of the most challenging aspects of love is learning to put the needs and desires of our partner above our own. True love is not self-seeking; it is willing to compromise and to prioritize the well-being of the other person.

In a romantic relationship, this means being willing to make sacrifices for the sake of the relationship. It involves listening to our partner's needs and desires, being flexible and open to their perspective, and working together to find solutions that benefit both partners. True love is not about getting our own way; it is about seeking the good of the other person.

5. Love is Not Irritable or Resentful: Irritability and resentment are signs of unresolved anger and frustration. When we are irritable, we are easily annoyed or provoked by the actions of others. Resentment, on the other hand, involves

holding onto past hurts and grievances, allowing them to fester and create bitterness.

In a romantic relationship, irritability and resentment can create a cycle of conflict and hurt. True love, however, is patient and forgiving. It involves letting go of past hurts, choosing to forgive our partner, and seeking reconciliation rather than holding onto anger. It also means being patient and understanding when our partner makes mistakes, and choosing to respond with grace rather than frustration.

6. Love Does Not Rejoice at Wrongdoing but Rejoices with the Truth: True love is rooted in truth and righteousness. It does not find pleasure in wrongdoing or injustice, but it rejoices in the truth and in what is good and right.

In a romantic relationship, this means being honest and transparent with our partner. It involves holding ourselves and our partner to a high standard of integrity and righteousness, and seeking to build a relationship that is based on truth, trust, and mutual respect. True love does not enable or condone harmful behavior; it seeks to promote what is good and right in the relationship.

7. Love Bears All Things, Believes All Things, Hopes All Things, Endures All Things: The final qualities that Paul mentions are perhaps the most challenging. True love is enduring and resilient. It is willing to bear the burdens and challenges of the relationship, to believe in the goodness of the other person, to hope for the best, and to endure through difficulties.

In a romantic relationship, these qualities are essential for building a lasting and fulfilling partnership. Love that bears all things is willing to support and uplift our partner, even in difficult times. Love that believes all things is willing to trust in the goodness and potential of our partner. Love that hopes all things is optimistic and forward-looking, always believing in the possibility of growth and improvement. And love that endures all things is steadfast and committed, willing to persevere through challenges and trials.

Human Love as a Reflection of God's Love

WHEN WE UNDERSTAND the characteristics of divine love as described in 1 Corinthians 13:4-7, we begin to see how human love, particularly in romantic relationships, is meant to be a reflection of God's love. This understanding challenges us to approach our relationships with a new perspective—one that is rooted in the love of God and that seeks to mirror His love in our interactions with others.

1. Love as a Reflection of God's Character: When we love others in the way that God loves us, we are reflecting His character and nature to the world. This is especially important in romantic relationships, where love is often most deeply felt and expressed. By embodying the qualities of divine love in our relationships, we become living testimonies of God's love, showing the world what true love looks like.

In John 13:35, Jesus tells His disciples, *"By this all people will know that you are my disciples, if you have love for one another."* Our love for others, especially in our closest relationships, is a powerful witness to the world of the transforming power of God's love. When our love reflects the characteristics of divine love, it points others to the source of that love—God Himself.

2. The Transformative Power of Love: One of the most remarkable aspects of God's love is its transformative power. God's love has the ability to change hearts, heal wounds, and bring about new life. When we love others with the same kind of love, we participate in this transformative work, helping to bring healing, growth, and renewal to our relationships.

In romantic relationships, this means that our love has the power to transform not only our partner but also ourselves. As we love our partner with patience, kindness, humility, and forgiveness, we create an environment where both partners can grow and flourish. This kind of love fosters deep intimacy, trust, and connection, and it allows the relationship to become a source of mutual support and encouragement.

3. Love as a Reflection of God's Covenant: God's love for us is covenantal—it is a committed, faithful, and enduring love that does not waver, even in the face of our failures and shortcomings. In romantic relationships, we are called to mirror this covenantal love by remaining committed to our partner, even when the relationship is challenging.

This kind of commitment is not based on fleeting emotions or circumstances; it is rooted in a deep and abiding love that reflects God's covenant with us. In marriage, this covenantal love is symbolized by the vows that partners make to one another, promising to love and cherish each other for better or worse, in sickness and in health, for as long as they both shall live.

These vows are a reflection of the covenant that God has made with us, and they serve as a reminder that true love is enduring and faithful.

4. Love as a Reflection of God's Sacrifice: The ultimate expression of God's love is found in the sacrificial death of Jesus Christ on the cross. In Romans 5:8, Paul writes, *"But God shows his love for us in that while we were still sinners, Christ died for us."* This sacrificial love is the foundation of our salvation, and it is the model for how we are to love others.

In romantic relationships, sacrificial love means being willing to put the needs and well-being of our partner above our own. It involves making sacrifices for the sake of the relationship, whether that means giving up our time, resources, or personal preferences. Sacrificial love is not about losing ourselves; it is about finding a deeper and more meaningful connection through self-giving and selflessness.

The Challenge and Reward of Reflecting God's Love

REFLECTING GOD'S LOVE in our romantic relationships is both a challenge and a reward. It requires us to move beyond our natural inclinations and to embrace a higher standard of love—one that is rooted in the character of God and empowered by the Holy Spirit. While this kind of love may be difficult to achieve, it is also deeply rewarding, bringing about growth, intimacy, and fulfillment in our relationships.

1. The Challenge of Selflessness: One of the greatest challenges of reflecting God's love is learning to be selfless. Our natural tendency is to focus on our own needs, desires, and preferences, often at the expense of others. However, true love, as described in 1 Corinthians 13:4-7, is selfless—it seeks the good of the other person above our own.

This selflessness is not something that comes naturally to us; it requires intentional effort and the work of the Holy Spirit in our hearts. It involves daily choosing to put our partner's needs above our own, to listen and understand their perspective, and to make sacrifices for the sake of the relationship. While this can be challenging, it is also deeply rewarding, as it leads to a deeper and more meaningful connection with our partner.

2. The Challenge of Forgiveness: Another significant challenge of reflecting God's love is learning to forgive. In any relationship, there will be times when

our partner hurts or disappoints us, whether intentionally or unintentionally. In these moments, our natural inclination may be to hold onto anger, resentment, or bitterness.

However, true love, as described in 1 Corinthians 13:5, is not resentful—it chooses to forgive and to let go of past hurts. This kind of forgiveness is not easy; it requires humility, grace, and a willingness to let go of our desire for retribution. Yet, when we choose to forgive, we create an environment of healing and reconciliation, allowing the relationship to grow and flourish.

3. The Reward of Intimacy: One of the most significant rewards of reflecting God's love in our relationships is the deep intimacy that it fosters. When we love our partner with patience, kindness, humility, and forgiveness, we create a safe and nurturing environment where both partners can be vulnerable and authentic.

This kind of intimacy goes beyond physical attraction or emotional connection; it is a deep and abiding bond that is rooted in mutual respect, trust, and love. It allows both partners to truly know and be known by each other, and it creates a foundation of stability and security that can withstand the challenges of life.

4. The Reward of Fulfillment: Reflecting God's love in our relationships also leads to a deep sense of fulfillment and purpose. When we love others in the way that God loves us, we are living in alignment with His will and His purposes for our lives. This kind of love brings joy, satisfaction, and a sense of meaning that goes beyond the superficial or temporary.

In romantic relationships, this fulfillment is experienced in the daily acts of love and service that we offer to our partner. It is found in the small moments of connection, the sacrifices made for the sake of the relationship, and the shared experiences of growth and learning. When our love reflects the love of God, our relationships become a source of deep and lasting fulfillment.

Practical Steps for Reflecting God's Love in Relationships

REFLECTING GOD'S LOVE in our romantic relationships requires intentionality and effort. Here are some practical steps to help you cultivate a love that mirrors the characteristics of divine love:

1. Deepen Your Relationship with God: The first step in reflecting God's love is to deepen your relationship with Him. Spend time in prayer, worship, and reading Scripture, allowing God's love to fill your heart and shape your perspective. As you grow in your relationship with God, His love will naturally flow through you and into your relationships.

2. Practice Patience and Kindness: In your daily interactions with your partner, practice patience and kindness. Choose to respond with grace rather than frustration, and seek to show compassion and understanding in your words and actions. These small acts of love can have a profound impact on your relationship.

3. Let Go of Envy and Pride: Be mindful of any feelings of envy or pride that may arise in your relationship. Choose to celebrate your partner's successes and blessings without feeling threatened or inferior. Focus on building up your partner rather than elevating yourself.

4. Prioritize Your Partner's Needs: Make a conscious effort to prioritize your partner's needs and desires above your own. This may involve making sacrifices or compromises for the sake of the relationship. By putting your partner's well-being first, you reflect the selflessness of God's love.

5. Choose Forgiveness: When conflicts or hurts arise in your relationship, choose to forgive rather than hold onto resentment. Forgiveness is a powerful act of love that can bring healing and reconciliation to your relationship. Let go of past grievances and seek to move forward with grace and understanding.

6. Commit to the Truth: Build your relationship on a foundation of truth and integrity. Be honest and transparent with your partner, and seek to promote what is good and right in your relationship. Avoid enabling harmful behavior and hold each other accountable to a high standard of righteousness.

Embrace the Challenges of Love: Recognize that love is not always easy; it requires endurance, resilience, and commitment. Embrace the challenges of love as opportunities for growth and learning, and trust that God is with you every step of the way.

Conclusion: The Beauty of Divine Love in Human Relationships

LOVE, WHEN ROOTED IN the characteristics of divine love, is one of the most beautiful and powerful expressions of God's presence in the world. Human love, especially in romantic relationships, has the potential to mirror God's love in profound ways, offering a glimpse of the divine to those around us.

1 Corinthians 13:4-7 provides a blueprint for how we are to love others—a love that is patient, kind, humble, selfless, forgiving, and enduring. When we reflect these qualities in our relationships, we not only build strong and fulfilling partnerships, but we also become living testimonies of God's love to the world.

As you navigate the journey of love and relationships, may you be encouraged to seek a love that reflects the heart of God. Let your love be a reflection of His patience, kindness, humility, and forgiveness. Embrace the challenges of love with grace and resilience, and trust that God is at work in your relationship, shaping it into a beautiful reflection of His love.

May your love for others, especially in your romantic relationships, be a powerful witness to the transforming power of God's love. And may you experience the deep joy, fulfillment, and intimacy that come from loving others as God has loved you—a love that is truly worth waiting for and that reflects the very nature of the divine.

Chapter 10: Sacrifice and Love

Theological Reflection: Reflect on the role of sacrifice in love and waiting. John 15:13 can be used to discuss the sacrificial nature of love, drawing parallels between Christ's sacrifice and the sacrifices made in waiting for true love.

Introduction: The Intersection of Love and Sacrifice

LOVE AND SACRIFICE are inextricably linked. From the beginning of time, the greatest acts of love have often been marked by profound sacrifices. Whether in the context of familial relationships, friendships, or romantic partnerships, sacrifice is the thread that weaves through the fabric of love, strengthening it, deepening it, and making it resilient. The highest expression of love often requires a willingness to give up something valuable—time, comfort, resources, or even personal desires—for the good of the one we love.

The ultimate example of sacrificial love is found in the life and death of Jesus Christ. In John 15:13, Jesus makes a profound statement about the nature of love: *"Greater love has no one than this, that someone lay down his life for his friends."* This declaration encapsulates the essence of sacrificial love—a love that is willing to give everything, even life itself, for the sake of another.

In the context of romantic relationships, the concept of sacrifice takes on a particularly poignant meaning. Waiting for true love, for the right person at the right time, often involves significant sacrifices. These sacrifices might include giving up immediate gratification, foregoing relationships that do not align with God's will, or enduring periods of loneliness and uncertainty. Yet, these sacrifices are not made in vain; they are a testament to the depth of our commitment to love that is genuine, lasting, and reflective of God's love for us.

In this chapter, we will explore the role of sacrifice in love and waiting, drawing parallels between Christ's sacrificial love and the sacrifices we make in the pursuit of true love. We will reflect on the theological significance of sacrifice, the challenges and rewards of sacrificial love, and the ways in which waiting for true love is itself an act of profound sacrifice.

The Theological Significance of Sacrifice

SACRIFICE IS A CENTRAL theme in Christian theology, rooted in the understanding of God's redemptive work through Jesus Christ. Throughout the Bible, sacrifice is portrayed as an essential aspect of worship, obedience, and love. From the Old Testament sacrifices offered by the Israelites to the ultimate sacrifice of Christ on the cross, the act of giving up something valuable to honor God and express love is a recurring motif.

1. Sacrifice in the Old Testament: In the Old Testament, sacrifice was a fundamental aspect of the covenant relationship between God and His people. The Israelites were instructed to offer sacrifices as a means of atoning for sin, expressing gratitude, and seeking God's favor. These sacrifices often involved the offering of animals, grains, or other valuable goods, symbolizing the worshiper's devotion and commitment to God.

The sacrificial system in the Old Testament foreshadowed the ultimate sacrifice that would be made by Jesus Christ. The sacrifices of animals were temporary and imperfect, pointing to the need for a perfect and final sacrifice that would atone for the sins of humanity once and for all.

2. The Sacrifice of Christ: The New Testament reveals that Jesus Christ is the fulfillment of the Old Testament sacrificial system. In Hebrews 10:10, we read, *"And by that will we have been sanctified through the offering of the body of Jesus Christ once for all."* Jesus' sacrifice on the cross was the ultimate act of love, offering Himself as the perfect and final sacrifice for the sins of the world.

This sacrificial love is the cornerstone of Christian faith and theology. It demonstrates the depth of God's love for humanity, a love that is willing to endure unimaginable suffering and death to bring about redemption and reconciliation. The cross is the ultimate symbol of sacrificial love, reminding us that true love is costly, but it is also transformative and redemptive.

3. Sacrifice as an Expression of Love: In Christian theology, sacrifice is not merely an act of giving something up; it is an expression of love. The sacrificial love of Christ is the model for how we are to love others. In Ephesians 5:1-2, Paul exhorts believers to *"Be imitators of God, as beloved children. And walk in love, as Christ loved us and gave himself up for us, a fragrant offering and sacrifice to God."* This passage highlights the connection between love and sacrifice, calling believers to love others in the same self-giving and sacrificial way that Christ loved us.

In the context of relationships, this means that true love is not self-seeking or conditional; it is willing to make sacrifices for the good of the other person. Whether it is sacrificing time, comfort, or personal desires, love that mirrors the love of Christ is characterized by a willingness to give up something valuable for the sake of the beloved.

The Role of Sacrifice in Romantic Relationships

IN ROMANTIC RELATIONSHIPS, sacrifice plays a crucial role in building and sustaining love. While the world often portrays love as a feeling or an emotion, Scripture teaches that love is an action—a deliberate choice to seek the good of another, even when it requires personal sacrifice.

1. Sacrifice as the Foundation of Commitment: One of the most important aspects of sacrifice in romantic relationships is its role in fostering commitment. Commitment is the foundation of any lasting relationship, and it is often tested by the need for sacrifice. When we choose to remain committed to our partner, even when it is difficult or inconvenient, we are demonstrating the depth of our love and our willingness to make sacrifices for the sake of the relationship.

In a world that often prioritizes personal fulfillment and instant gratification, the willingness to make sacrifices for the sake of love can be countercultural. Yet, it is precisely this willingness to sacrifice that sets true love apart from superficial or self-centered relationships. Sacrificial love is not about getting what we want; it is about giving of ourselves for the good of the other person and for the flourishing of the relationship.

2. Sacrifice in the Face of Challenges: Every romantic relationship will face challenges and difficulties, whether they are external circumstances, personal struggles, or relational conflicts. In these moments, the strength of the

relationship is often determined by the willingness of both partners to make sacrifices for the sake of resolving the issue and preserving the relationship.

Sacrifice in the face of challenges might involve setting aside personal pride to apologize, making time for the relationship despite a busy schedule, or supporting a partner through a difficult season. These acts of sacrifice demonstrate a commitment to the relationship and a willingness to prioritize the well-being of the other person above our own comfort or convenience.

3. Sacrifice as an Act of Trust: Sacrifice in a romantic relationship also requires trust—trust in God's plan for the relationship, trust in the other person's intentions, and trust in the process of growth and development. When we make sacrifices for the sake of love, we are often stepping into the unknown, relinquishing control, and placing our trust in something greater than ourselves.

This trust is particularly important in the context of waiting for true love. Waiting often involves significant sacrifices, such as foregoing relationships that do not align with God's will, enduring periods of loneliness, and resisting the temptation to settle for less than God's best. These sacrifices require trust in God's timing and His plan for our lives, believing that the sacrifices we make now will ultimately lead to a deeper and more fulfilling love in the future.

Parallels Between Christ's Sacrifice and Sacrificial Love in Relationships

THE SACRIFICIAL LOVE of Christ, as demonstrated on the cross, serves as the ultimate model for how we are to love others, particularly in romantic relationships. While the sacrifices we make in our relationships may not be as dramatic or life-altering as Christ's sacrifice, they are nonetheless significant and reflective of the same self-giving love.

1. The Willingness to Lay Down One's Life: In John 15:13, Jesus states, *"Greater love has no one than this, that someone lay down his life for his friends."* While most of us will not be called to literally lay down our lives for our loved ones, this statement highlights the extent of sacrificial love—the willingness to give up everything, even life itself, for the sake of another.

In romantic relationships, this willingness to lay down one's life is reflected in the everyday sacrifices we make for our partner. It might involve giving up personal dreams or ambitions to support our partner's goals, sacrificing time and energy to care for our partner in times of need, or making difficult decisions for the good of the relationship. These sacrifices, though they may seem small in comparison to Christ's sacrifice, are nonetheless expressions of the same self-giving love that Jesus exemplified.

2. The Joy of Sacrificial Love: One of the most remarkable aspects of Christ's sacrifice is that it was motivated by love and accompanied by joy. Hebrews 12:2 tells us that Jesus, *"for the joy that was set before him endured the cross, despising the shame, and is seated at the right hand of the throne of God."* The joy that Jesus experienced was not in the suffering itself, but in the knowledge that His sacrifice would bring about the redemption of humanity and the fulfillment of God's plan.

In romantic relationships, sacrificial love is also accompanied by joy—the joy of knowing that our sacrifices are contributing to the growth and flourishing of the relationship. While sacrifice may involve hardship or discomfort, it also brings a deep sense of fulfillment and purpose, knowing that we are loving our partner in a way that reflects God's love for us. This joy is a powerful motivator, enabling us to endure the challenges of sacrifice with grace and gratitude.

3. The Redemptive Power of Sacrifice: Christ's sacrifice on the cross was the ultimate act of redemption, bringing about the forgiveness of sins and the reconciliation of humanity with God. This redemptive power is also at work in our relationships when we make sacrifices for the sake of love.

In romantic relationships, sacrifices can have a transformative and redemptive effect, healing wounds, restoring trust, and deepening intimacy. For example, the sacrifice of forgiveness can bring about reconciliation after a conflict, the sacrifice of time can strengthen the bond between partners, and the sacrifice of personal desires can lead to greater unity and harmony in the relationship. These acts of sacrificial love not only benefit the relationship but also reflect the redemptive love of Christ, pointing to the deeper spiritual significance of our love for one another.

The Challenges of Sacrificial Love

WHILE SACRIFICIAL LOVE is beautiful and transformative, it is not without its challenges. In a culture that often prioritizes self-fulfillment and individualism, the idea of making sacrifices for the sake of love can be difficult to embrace. Sacrificial love requires us to move beyond our natural inclinations and to embrace a higher standard of love—one that is rooted in selflessness, humility, and trust in God.

1. The Challenge of Self-Denial: One of the greatest challenges of sacrificial love is the call to deny ourselves—to set aside our own desires, preferences, and comfort for the sake of the other person. This self-denial is countercultural, as it goes against the prevailing message that we should always prioritize our own happiness and fulfillment.

However, Jesus calls His followers to a different way of life, one that is marked by self-denial and sacrificial love. In Matthew 16:24-25, Jesus says, *"If anyone would come after me, let him deny himself and take up his cross and follow me. For whoever would save his life will lose it, but whoever loses his life for my sake will find it."* This call to take up our cross and follow Jesus is a call to embrace the way of sacrificial love, even when it requires us to give up something valuable.

In romantic relationships, this might mean making difficult sacrifices, such as giving up a career opportunity to be with our partner, sacrificing personal time to care for our partner, or relinquishing control over certain aspects of the relationship. While these sacrifices may be challenging, they are also opportunities to grow in love and to reflect the self-giving love of Christ.

2. The Challenge of Vulnerability: Sacrificial love also requires vulnerability—the willingness to open ourselves up to the possibility of hurt, disappointment, or rejection. When we make sacrifices for the sake of love, we are often placing ourselves in a position of vulnerability, trusting that our sacrifices will be received with gratitude and reciprocated with love.

However, vulnerability can be frightening, especially in a world where we are often encouraged to protect ourselves and avoid getting hurt. Yet, it is precisely this vulnerability that allows for deep intimacy and connection in a relationship. When we are willing to make sacrifices and to be vulnerable with our partner, we create an environment of trust and openness, where both partners can grow and flourish.

3. The Challenge of Perseverance: Sacrificial love also requires perseverance—the ability to continue loving and making sacrifices even when it is difficult or when the relationship is going through a challenging season. Perseverance in love is not about enduring hardship for the sake of suffering; it is about remaining committed to the relationship and to the well-being of the other person, even when it requires sustained effort and sacrifice.

In 1 Corinthians 13:7, Paul writes that love *"bears all things, believes all things, hopes all things, endures all things."* This endurance is a key aspect of sacrificial love, enabling us to weather the storms of life and to remain steadfast in our commitment to love and to our partner. While perseverance in love can be challenging, it is also deeply rewarding, as it leads to a relationship that is resilient, strong, and built on a foundation of sacrificial love.

The Rewards of Sacrificial Love

DESPITE THE CHALLENGES of sacrificial love, the rewards are abundant. When we choose to love sacrificially, we experience the deep joy, fulfillment, and growth that come from giving of ourselves for the sake of another. These rewards are not only experienced in the context of our relationships but also in our spiritual lives, as we grow closer to God and become more like Christ.

1. The Joy of Deep Connection: One of the most significant rewards of sacrificial love is the deep connection and intimacy that it fosters in a relationship. When both partners are willing to make sacrifices for the sake of the relationship, they create an environment of mutual trust, respect, and love. This deep connection goes beyond surface-level attraction or emotional connection; it is a bond that is built on shared sacrifices and a commitment to the well-being of the other person.

This deep connection is not only fulfilling but also stabilizing, providing a strong foundation for the relationship to grow and flourish. Sacrificial love leads to a relationship that is resilient and enduring, capable of withstanding the challenges and trials of life.

2. The Fulfillment of Living Out God's Love: When we love sacrificially, we are living out the love of God in our relationships. This brings a deep sense of

fulfillment and purpose, as we are participating in the work of God's kingdom and reflecting His love to the world. Sacrificial love is not just about giving up something for the sake of the other person; it is about embodying the love of Christ and living in alignment with God's will.

This fulfillment is experienced not only in our relationships but also in our spiritual lives, as we grow closer to God and become more like Christ. Sacrificial love is a powerful way to deepen our relationship with God, as it requires us to rely on His strength, guidance, and love.

3. The Growth of Personal Character: Sacrificial love also leads to personal growth and the development of Christ-like character. When we choose to make sacrifices for the sake of love, we are cultivating qualities such as humility, patience, perseverance, and selflessness. These qualities are not only essential for healthy relationships but also for our spiritual growth and maturity.

As we grow in sacrificial love, we become more like Christ, reflecting His character and love in our relationships and in the world. This personal growth is one of the most significant rewards of sacrificial love, as it leads to a deeper and more meaningful relationship with God and with others.

4. The Assurance of God's Blessings: Finally, sacrificial love brings with it the assurance of God's blessings. Throughout Scripture, we see that God honors and blesses those who love sacrificially, as they are living in alignment with His will and reflecting His love to the world.

In Romans 12:1, Paul writes, *"I appeal to you therefore, brothers, by the mercies of God, to present your bodies as a living sacrifice, holy and acceptable to God, which is your spiritual worship."* When we offer our lives as a living sacrifice to God, including our relationships and the sacrifices we make for the sake of love, we are worshiping God and aligning ourselves with His purposes. This act of worship brings with it the assurance of God's presence, guidance, and blessings in our lives.

Practical Steps for Cultivating Sacrificial Love

CULTIVATING SACRIFICIAL love in our relationships requires intentionality, effort, and a deep reliance on God's strength and guidance.

Here are some practical steps to help you develop and maintain a love that is characterized by sacrifice:

1. Seek God's Guidance: Begin by seeking God's guidance in your relationships and in your understanding of sacrificial love. Spend time in prayer, asking God to reveal areas in your life where you may need to make sacrifices for the sake of love. Ask for the Holy Spirit's help in cultivating a heart of selflessness and humility.

2. Practice Self-Denial: Look for opportunities to practice self-denial in your daily life. This might involve making small sacrifices for the sake of your partner, such as giving up personal time to spend with them, sacrificing your comfort to meet their needs, or putting their desires above your own. These acts of self-denial, though they may seem small, are powerful expressions of sacrificial love.

3. Embrace Vulnerability: Be willing to embrace vulnerability in your relationships. This means being open and honest with your partner about your feelings, needs, and struggles, and being willing to make sacrifices for the sake of the relationship, even when it involves taking risks or stepping out of your comfort zone.

4. Persevere in Love: Cultivate perseverance in your relationships, especially in times of difficulty or challenge. Choose to remain committed to your partner and to the relationship, even when it requires sustained effort and sacrifice. Trust that God is at work in your relationship, and that your sacrifices are contributing to the growth and flourishing of your love.

5. Reflect on Christ's Sacrifice: Regularly reflect on the sacrificial love of Christ, as demonstrated on the cross. Meditate on Scriptures that speak to the depth of Christ's love and His willingness to lay down His life for us. Allow this reflection to inspire and motivate you to love others in the same self-giving and sacrificial way.

Trust in God's Timing: Finally, trust in God's timing for your relationships. If you are waiting for true love, trust that the sacrifices you are making now—whether they involve waiting, resisting temptation, or foregoing relationships that do not align with God's will—are not in vain. Trust that God is preparing you and your future partner for a love that is deep, fulfilling, and reflective of His love.

Conclusion: The Beauty and Power of Sacrificial Love

SACRIFICIAL LOVE IS one of the most beautiful and powerful expressions of God's love in the world. It is a love that is willing to give up something valuable for the sake of another, a love that is rooted in selflessness, humility, and trust in God. In romantic relationships, sacrificial love is essential for building and sustaining a deep, fulfilling, and enduring bond.

John 15:13 reminds us that "Greater love has no one than this, that someone lay down his life for his friends." While we may not be called to literally lay down our lives for our loved ones, we are called to love sacrificially in our daily lives, making sacrifices for the sake of our partner and for the flourishing of the relationship.

As you navigate the journey of love and relationships, may you be encouraged to embrace the call to sacrificial love. Seek God's guidance, practice self-denial, embrace vulnerability, persevere in love, and trust in God's timing. Reflect on the sacrificial love of Christ, and let it inspire you to love others in the same self-giving and sacrificial way.

May your love for others, especially in your romantic relationships, be a powerful reflection of God's love—a love that is deep, enduring, and transformative. And may you experience the profound joy, fulfillment, and growth that come from living out the sacrificial love of Christ in your relationships.

Chapter 11: Forgiveness and Reconciliation

Theological Reflection: Explore the themes of forgiveness and reconciliation in relationships. Use Ephesians 4:32 to discuss how forgiveness is essential in any loving relationship and how waiting can lead to reconciliation.

Introduction: The Healing Power of Forgiveness

FORGIVENESS AND RECONCILIATION are central themes in the Christian faith, deeply rooted in the character and work of God. They are also essential components of any healthy, loving relationship. Whether in friendships, family dynamics, or romantic partnerships, the ability to forgive and seek reconciliation is crucial for the growth, healing, and longevity of relationships. Without forgiveness, relationships are prone to bitterness, resentment, and division. Without reconciliation, relationships can become fractured, leading to isolation and a loss of connection.

The Bible speaks extensively about the importance of forgiveness, not only as an act of grace towards others but also as a reflection of God's forgiveness towards us. In Ephesians 4:32, the Apostle Paul exhorts believers to *"Be kind to one another, tenderhearted, forgiving one another, as God in Christ forgave you."* This verse highlights the dual nature of forgiveness: it is both a command to forgive others and a reminder of the forgiveness we have received through Christ. Forgiveness is not merely an option in a loving relationship; it is a necessity, rooted in the example set by Christ.

Reconciliation, closely tied to forgiveness, is the process of restoring broken relationships. It involves more than just forgiving someone; it is about rebuilding trust, healing wounds, and re-establishing a sense of connection and unity. While forgiveness can be granted by one person, reconciliation requires the willingness and effort of both parties to work towards healing and restoration.

In this chapter, we will explore the themes of forgiveness and reconciliation in relationships, drawing from Ephesians 4:32 to understand how these concepts are essential in any loving relationship. We will reflect on the theological significance of forgiveness, the challenges and rewards of practicing forgiveness, and the ways in which waiting—whether for the right time, for the right person, or for healing—can lead to reconciliation.

The Theological Foundation of Forgiveness

FORGIVENESS IS A FUNDAMENTAL aspect of the Christian faith, rooted in the understanding of God's nature and His redemptive work through Jesus Christ. The Bible teaches that God is a forgiving God, who is merciful, compassionate, and slow to anger. His forgiveness is not contingent upon our worthiness but is an expression of His grace and love. This divine forgiveness serves as the model for how we are to forgive others.

1. God's Forgiveness of Humanity: Throughout Scripture, we see numerous examples of God's forgiveness towards humanity. From the Old Testament to the New Testament, God's willingness to forgive is evident, even in the face of repeated sin and rebellion. In Exodus 34:6-7, God reveals His character to Moses, saying, *"The Lord, the Lord, a God merciful and gracious, slow to anger, and abounding in steadfast love and faithfulness, keeping steadfast love for thousands, forgiving iniquity and transgression and sin."* This passage highlights the compassionate and forgiving nature of God, who is always ready to extend mercy to those who repent.

The ultimate expression of God's forgiveness is found in the life, death, and resurrection of Jesus Christ. In Colossians 2:13-14, Paul writes, *"And you, who were dead in your trespasses and the uncircumcision of your flesh, God made alive together with him, having forgiven us all our trespasses, by canceling the record of debt that stood against us with its legal demands. This he set aside, nailing it to the cross."* Through Christ's sacrificial death on the cross, God forgave the sins of humanity, offering redemption and reconciliation to all who believe.

2. The Command to Forgive: Because we have received such great forgiveness from God, we are called to extend that same forgiveness to others. Jesus makes this clear in the Lord's Prayer, where He teaches His disciples to pray, *"And forgive us our debts, as we also have forgiven our debtors"* (Matthew 6:12). He goes on to emphasize the importance of forgiveness, saying, *"For if you forgive others their trespasses, your heavenly Father will also forgive you, but if you do not forgive others their trespasses, neither will your Father forgive your trespasses"* (Matthew 6:14-15).

This command to forgive is not just a suggestion; it is a reflection of the grace and mercy that we have received from God. When we forgive others, we are participating in the redemptive work of God, reflecting His love and compassion to the world. Forgiveness is an essential aspect of discipleship, and it is a powerful witness to the transformative power of God's grace.

3. The Role of the Holy Spirit in Forgiveness: Forgiving others, especially when we have been deeply hurt, is not something we can do on our own. It requires the work of the Holy Spirit in our hearts, transforming us and enabling us to extend grace to others. In Ephesians 4:30-32, Paul writes, *"And do not grieve the Holy Spirit of God, by whom you were sealed for the day of redemption. Let all bitterness and wrath and anger and clamor and slander be put away from you, along with all malice. Be kind to one another, tenderhearted, forgiving one another, as God in Christ forgave you."*

The Holy Spirit empowers us to let go of bitterness, anger, and resentment, replacing them with kindness, compassion, and forgiveness. As we yield to the work of the Holy Spirit, we are transformed into the likeness of Christ, who forgave even those who crucified Him, saying, *"Father, forgive them, for they know not what they do"* (Luke 23:34).

Forgiveness in Romantic Relationships

IN ROMANTIC RELATIONSHIPS, forgiveness is essential for maintaining harmony, trust, and intimacy. No relationship is without its challenges, misunderstandings, or conflicts, and without forgiveness, these issues can lead to bitterness, resentment, and ultimately, the breakdown of the relationship. Forgiveness, however, allows for healing, growth, and the deepening of the bond between partners.

1. Forgiveness as a Choice: Forgiveness is not merely an emotion; it is a deliberate choice to let go of anger, resentment, and the desire for revenge. In a romantic relationship, this choice is crucial for maintaining a healthy and loving connection. When we choose to forgive our partner, we are prioritizing the relationship and the well-being of the other person over our own hurt or pride.

Forgiveness in a relationship does not mean ignoring or excusing hurtful behavior. Instead, it involves acknowledging the pain, addressing the issue, and then choosing to release the negative emotions associated with it. This choice to forgive creates an environment where both partners can feel safe, valued, and respected, even in the midst of conflict.

2. The Importance of Mutual Forgiveness: For a romantic relationship to thrive, both partners must be willing to forgive each other. Mutual forgiveness fosters an environment of grace, where both individuals recognize their own imperfections and are willing to extend grace to their partner. This mutual forgiveness builds trust and creates a foundation for deeper intimacy and connection.

In Ephesians 4:2, Paul urges believers to *"be completely humble and gentle; be patient, bearing with one another in love."* This call to bear with one another in love is especially important in romantic relationships, where close proximity and deep emotional connection can sometimes lead to misunderstandings or conflicts. By practicing mutual forgiveness, partners demonstrate their commitment to the relationship and their willingness to work through challenges together.

3. The Role of Communication in Forgiveness: Effective communication is essential for forgiveness and reconciliation in a relationship. Without open and honest communication, misunderstandings can fester, and hurt feelings can go unaddressed. When conflicts arise, it is important for both partners to communicate their feelings, listen to each other's perspectives, and work together to find a resolution.

In James 1:19, we are instructed to *"be quick to hear, slow to speak, slow to anger."* This verse highlights the importance of listening before reacting, a principle that is crucial for forgiveness and reconciliation. By listening to our partner's perspective and expressing our own feelings with gentleness and respect, we create an environment where forgiveness can flourish.

4. Forgiveness as a Path to Healing: Forgiveness is a powerful tool for healing in a relationship. When we forgive, we release the emotional and spiritual burdens that come with holding onto anger and resentment. This release allows for healing to take place, both individually and within the relationship.

Forgiveness does not necessarily mean forgetting the hurt or returning to the way things were before. Instead, it involves acknowledging the pain, working through it, and then moving forward with a renewed commitment to the relationship. This process of forgiveness and healing can lead to a deeper, more resilient bond between partners.

The Process of Reconciliation

WHILE FORGIVENESS IS a crucial first step in healing a relationship, reconciliation goes a step further. Reconciliation is the process of restoring the relationship to a state of unity and harmony after a conflict or breach has occurred. It involves rebuilding trust, re-establishing communication, and working together to heal the wounds that have been inflicted.

1. The Necessity of Repentance: Reconciliation cannot occur without genuine repentance from the person who has caused the hurt. Repentance involves acknowledging the wrong, taking responsibility for it, and making a commitment to change. This process of repentance is essential for rebuilding trust and creating a foundation for reconciliation.

In Luke 17:3-4, Jesus teaches about the relationship between forgiveness and repentance: *"Pay attention to yourselves! If your brother sins, rebuke him, and if he repents, forgive him, and if he sins against you seven times in the day, and turns to you seven times, saying, 'I repent,' you must forgive him."* This passage highlights the importance of repentance in the process of forgiveness and reconciliation. Without repentance, reconciliation may be difficult or even impossible, as trust cannot be rebuilt without a genuine acknowledgment of wrongdoing.

2. The Role of Time in Reconciliation: Reconciliation is often a process that takes time. While forgiveness can be granted in a moment, reconciliation may require ongoing effort and patience as both parties work through their emotions, rebuild trust, and re-establish the relationship. This process may

involve multiple conversations, counseling, or simply allowing time for healing to take place.

In some cases, waiting is necessary for reconciliation to occur. This waiting period allows both individuals to reflect, heal, and gain perspective on the situation. It also provides an opportunity for God to work in their hearts, bringing about transformation and growth that can lead to a stronger and healthier relationship.

3. The Importance of Humility in Reconciliation: Humility is essential for both forgiveness and reconciliation. It requires both parties to set aside their pride, acknowledge their own faults, and be willing to work towards healing and restoration. In Philippians 2:3-4, Paul exhorts believers to *"do nothing from selfish ambition or conceit, but in humility count others more significant than yourselves. Let each of you look not only to his own interests but also to the interests of others."*

This call to humility is particularly important in the process of reconciliation, where both parties must be willing to prioritize the relationship and the well-being of the other person over their own ego or desire to be right. Humility allows for genuine repentance, open communication, and a willingness to work together towards reconciliation.

4. The Role of Grace in Reconciliation: Reconciliation is ultimately an act of grace—both the grace that we extend to others and the grace that we receive from God. Grace is the unmerited favor of God, and it is the foundation of our ability to forgive and seek reconciliation with others.

In 2 Corinthians 5:18-19, Paul writes, *"All this is from God, who through Christ reconciled us to himself and gave us the ministry of reconciliation; that is, in Christ God was reconciling the world to himself, not counting their trespasses against them, and entrusting to us the message of reconciliation."* This passage highlights the connection between God's reconciliation with humanity and our call to be agents of reconciliation in our relationships.

As recipients of God's grace, we are called to extend that same grace to others, seeking reconciliation even when it is difficult or costly. This grace enables us to move beyond the pain of the past and to work towards a future of healing, unity, and love.

The Challenges of Forgiveness and Reconciliation

FORGIVENESS AND RECONCILIATION, while essential for healthy relationships, are not without their challenges. They require us to move beyond our natural inclinations and to embrace a higher standard of love, grace, and humility. These challenges are opportunities for growth, both personally and within the relationship.

1. The Challenge of Letting Go: One of the greatest challenges of forgiveness is the difficulty of letting go of the hurt, anger, and resentment that we may feel towards someone who has wronged us. These emotions can be powerful, and they can create barriers to forgiveness and reconciliation.

In Matthew 18:21-22, Peter asks Jesus, *"Lord, how often will my brother sin against me, and I forgive him? As many as seven times?"* Jesus responds, *"I do not say to you seven times, but seventy-seven times."* This response highlights the limitless nature of forgiveness, but it also underscores the challenge of continually letting go of the pain and choosing to forgive.

Letting go does not mean ignoring the hurt or pretending that it did not happen. Instead, it involves releasing the emotional hold that the hurt has on us and choosing to move forward with grace and compassion. This process may take time and may require the help of the Holy Spirit to truly let go and forgive.

2. The Challenge of Vulnerability: Forgiveness and reconciliation require vulnerability—the willingness to open ourselves up to the possibility of being hurt again. This vulnerability can be frightening, especially if we have been deeply wounded in the past.

However, vulnerability is also a key component of intimacy and connection in a relationship. Without vulnerability, we cannot truly experience the depth of love, trust, and connection that comes from forgiveness and reconciliation. In 2 Corinthians 12:9, Paul shares God's response to his struggles: *"My grace is sufficient for you, for my power is made perfect in weakness."* This verse reminds us that in our vulnerability and weakness, God's grace and strength are at work, enabling us to forgive and seek reconciliation.

3. The Challenge of Trust: Rebuilding trust is one of the most difficult aspects of reconciliation. Trust is easily broken, but it can take time to rebuild. This process requires consistent effort, honesty, and a willingness to work through the challenges together.

In Proverbs 3:5-6, we are reminded to *"Trust in the Lord with all your heart, and do not lean on your own understanding. In all your ways acknowledge him, and he will make straight your paths."* This verse highlights the importance of placing our trust in God, even as we work to rebuild trust in our human relationships. Trusting in God's guidance and timing can help us navigate the challenges of rebuilding trust in our relationships.

4. The Challenge of Moving Forward: Once forgiveness has been granted and reconciliation has begun, the challenge remains to move forward in the relationship without holding onto the past. This can be difficult, especially if the hurt was deep or the breach was significant.

In Philippians 3:13-14, Paul writes, *"But one thing I do: forgetting what lies behind and straining forward to what lies ahead, I press on toward the goal for the prize of the upward call of God in Christ Jesus."* This passage encourages us to focus on the future, rather than dwelling on the past. Moving forward in a relationship after forgiveness and reconciliation involves a commitment to building a new foundation of trust, love, and respect, rather than allowing the past to define the relationship.

The Rewards of Forgiveness and Reconciliation

WHILE FORGIVENESS AND reconciliation can be challenging, the rewards are profound and transformative. These rewards are experienced both within the relationship and in our spiritual lives, as we grow closer to God and become more like Christ.

1. The Joy of Restoration: One of the most significant rewards of forgiveness and reconciliation is the joy of restoration. When a relationship is restored after a breach, there is a deep sense of joy, relief, and gratitude. This restoration brings a renewed sense of connection, intimacy, and trust, allowing the relationship to grow and flourish.

In Luke 15, Jesus tells the parable of the prodigal son, a story that beautifully illustrates the joy of reconciliation. When the prodigal son returns home after squandering his inheritance, his father runs to him, embraces him, and celebrates his return with a feast. This story highlights the joy that comes from reconciliation, both in our relationship with God and in our human relationships.

2. The Freedom of Letting Go: Forgiveness brings with it the freedom of letting go—letting go of the anger, resentment, and bitterness that can weigh us down and hold us back. When we forgive, we release these burdens and experience the freedom and peace that come from living in grace.

In Matthew 11:28-30, Jesus invites us to come to Him with our burdens: *"Come to me, all who labor and are heavy laden, and I will give you rest. Take my yoke upon you, and learn from me, for I am gentle and lowly in heart, and you will find rest for your souls. For my yoke is easy, and my burden is light."* This invitation to rest in Jesus reminds us that forgiveness is not just about releasing others from their debt; it is also about releasing ourselves from the burdens of anger and bitterness.

3. The Growth of Personal Character: Forgiveness and reconciliation also lead to personal growth and the development of Christ-like character. When we choose to forgive and seek reconciliation, we are cultivating qualities such as humility, patience, compassion, and grace. These qualities are essential for healthy relationships and for our spiritual growth and maturity.

In Colossians 3:12-14, Paul writes, *"Put on then, as God's chosen ones, holy and beloved, compassionate hearts, kindness, humility, meekness, and patience, bearing with one another and, if one has a complaint against another, forgiving each other; as the Lord has forgiven you, so you also must forgive. And above all these put on love, which binds everything together in perfect harmony."* This passage highlights the connection between forgiveness and the development of Christ-like character, encouraging us to embody these qualities in our relationships.

4. The Assurance of God's Blessings: Finally, forgiveness and reconciliation bring with them the assurance of God's blessings. When we forgive others and seek reconciliation, we are living in alignment with God's will and reflecting His love and grace to the world. This act of obedience brings with it the assurance of God's presence, guidance, and blessings in our lives.

In Matthew 5:9, Jesus says, "Blessed are the peacemakers, for they shall be called sons of God." This verse reminds us that when we seek peace and reconciliation in our relationships, we are living as children of God, reflecting His character and participating in His redemptive work in the world.

Practical Steps for Practicing Forgiveness and Reconciliation

PRACTICING FORGIVENESS and reconciliation in our relationships requires intentionality, effort, and a deep reliance on God's strength and guidance. Here are some practical steps to help you cultivate these essential qualities in your relationships:

1. Seek God's Guidance: Begin by seeking God's guidance in your relationships and in your understanding of forgiveness and reconciliation. Spend time in prayer, asking God to reveal areas in your life where you may need to forgive or seek reconciliation. Ask for the Holy Spirit's help in cultivating a heart of grace, humility, and compassion.

2. Acknowledge the Hurt: Forgiveness begins with acknowledging the hurt and the impact it has had on you. Take time to reflect on the situation and to understand your emotions. This acknowledgment is an important first step in the process of healing and forgiveness.

3. Choose to Forgive: Remember that forgiveness is a choice, not an emotion. Choose to forgive the person who has hurt you, even if you do not feel like it. This choice is an act of obedience to God and a reflection of the forgiveness you have received through Christ.

4. Communicate Openly: If possible, communicate openly with the person who has hurt you. Share your feelings and perspectives with gentleness and respect, and be willing to listen to their side of the story. This open communication is essential for both forgiveness and reconciliation.

5. Seek Reconciliation: If the other person is willing, work towards reconciliation. This may involve rebuilding trust, re-establishing communication, and working together to heal the wounds that have been inflicted. Be patient and allow time for the process of reconciliation to unfold.

6. Rely on God's Strength: Forgiveness and reconciliation can be challenging, but remember that you do not have to do it on your own. Rely on God's strength, guidance, and grace as you work through the process. Trust that God is at work in your heart and in the relationship, bringing about healing and restoration.

7. Move Forward in Love: Once forgiveness has been granted and reconciliation has begun, commit to moving forward in love. Let go of the

past and focus on building a new foundation of trust, respect, and love in the relationship. Remember that love is the bond that holds everything together in perfect harmony.

Conclusion: The Power of Forgiveness and Reconciliation

FORGIVENESS AND RECONCILIATION are powerful expressions of God's love and grace in our relationships. They are essential for healing, growth, and the deepening of our connections with others. In Ephesians 4:32, we are reminded to "Be kind to one another, tenderhearted, forgiving one another, as God in Christ forgave you." This call to forgiveness is not just a command; it is an invitation to participate in the redemptive work of God, reflecting His love and grace to the world.

As you navigate the journey of love and relationships, may you be encouraged to embrace the call to forgiveness and reconciliation. Seek God's guidance, practice humility, and rely on the Holy Spirit as you work towards healing and restoration in your relationships. Remember that forgiveness is not just about releasing others from their debt; it is also about releasing yourself from the burdens of anger and bitterness.

May your relationships be marked by the grace, love, and compassion that come from a heart transformed by God's forgiveness. And may you experience the profound joy, freedom, and growth that come from living out the principles of forgiveness and reconciliation in your relationships.

Chapter 12: Hope in God's Promises

Theological Reflection: Discuss how hope sustains us while waiting for love. Romans 15:13 can be the foundation for reflecting on the hope that comes from believing in God's promises for a fulfilled and loving relationship.

Introduction: The Power of Hope

HOPE IS A POWERFUL and sustaining force in the human experience. It is the belief that something good and meaningful lies ahead, even in the face of uncertainty or difficulty. In the Christian faith, hope is not merely wishful thinking or blind optimism; it is rooted in the promises of God, who is faithful, sovereign, and loving. The hope we have in God's promises gives us strength, courage, and perseverance, especially in times of waiting.

One of the most challenging seasons of waiting is the period before finding true love or before a relationship comes to fruition. During this time, it is easy to become discouraged, frustrated, or even doubtful about the future. However, the Bible encourages us to hold onto hope, trusting that God's plans for us are good and that He is working all things together for our benefit.

Romans 15:13 is a verse that encapsulates the essence of Christian hope: *"May the God of hope fill you with all joy and peace in believing, so that by the power of the Holy Spirit you may abound in hope."* This verse reminds us that God is the source of our hope, and that through the Holy Spirit, we can experience an abundance of hope that brings joy and peace, even in the midst of waiting.

In this chapter, we will explore the role of hope in sustaining us while waiting for love. We will reflect on the theological significance of hope, the challenges of maintaining hope in difficult times, and the ways in which God's promises provide a foundation for our hope. Drawing from Romans 15:13, we will consider how hope in God's promises can lead to a fulfilled and loving relationship, and how it can transform our perspective and our lives.

The Theological Foundation of Hope

HOPE IS A CENTRAL THEME in Christian theology, deeply connected to the character of God and His redemptive work in the world. The Bible presents hope not as a vague or uncertain expectation, but as a confident assurance in God's promises and His faithfulness.

1. God as the Source of Hope: The foundation of Christian hope is God Himself. Throughout Scripture, God is portrayed as the ultimate source of hope, the one who holds the future in His hands and who is faithful to fulfill His promises. In Jeremiah 29:11, God declares, *"For I know the plans I have for you, declares the Lord, plans for welfare and not for evil, to give you a future and a hope."* This verse highlights the connection between God's sovereignty and the hope that we have in Him.

The New Testament further reinforces this understanding of God as the source of hope. In 1 Peter 1:3, Peter writes, *"Blessed be the God and Father of our Lord Jesus Christ! According to his great mercy, he has caused us to be born again to a living hope through the resurrection of Jesus Christ from the dead."* This living hope is not based on our circumstances or our own efforts; it is rooted in the resurrection of Christ and the new life that we have in Him.

2. The Promises of God: The hope that sustains us in times of waiting is grounded in the promises of God. Throughout the Bible, God makes numerous promises to His people—promises of provision, protection, guidance, and ultimately, eternal life. These promises are not empty or uncertain; they are backed by the character of God, who is faithful and true.

One of the most significant promises that God makes to His people is the promise of His presence. In Deuteronomy 31:8, Moses reassures the Israelites, *"It is the Lord who goes before you. He will be with you; he will not leave you or forsake you. Do not fear or be dismayed."* This promise of God's constant presence is a source of hope and comfort, especially in times of waiting.

In the New Testament, we see the fulfillment of God's promises in the person of Jesus Christ. Jesus is the embodiment of God's promises, the one through whom all of God's promises find their "Yes" and "Amen" (2 Corinthians 1:20). As we place our hope in Christ, we can trust that God's promises will be fulfilled in our lives, both now and in the future.

3. The Role of the Holy Spirit: The Holy Spirit plays a crucial role in sustaining our hope. In Romans 15:13, Paul prays that God would fill believers with joy and peace in believing, so that they may abound in hope by the power of the Holy Spirit. The Holy Spirit is the one who enables us to experience the fullness of hope, even in difficult circumstances.

The Holy Spirit works in our hearts to remind us of God's promises, to strengthen our faith, and to produce in us the fruit of hope. In Romans 8:24-25, Paul writes, *"For in this hope we were saved. Now hope that is seen is not hope. For who hopes for what he sees? But if we hope for what we do not see, we wait for it with patience."* The Holy Spirit gives us the patience and endurance to wait for what we cannot yet see, trusting that God is faithful and that His promises will come to pass

Hope in the Context of Waiting for Love

WAITING FOR LOVE, WHETHER it be the right person, the right time, or the deepening of an existing relationship, can be one of the most challenging experiences in life. The uncertainty, the longing, and the fear of disappointment can all weigh heavily on our hearts. However, it is precisely in these moments of waiting that hope becomes most vital.

1. The Challenge of Waiting: Waiting for love often involves a tension between desire and patience. On one hand, we have a natural desire for connection, companionship, and intimacy. On the other hand, we are called to wait for God's timing and to trust that His plans for us are good.

This tension can lead to feelings of frustration, impatience, and even doubt. We may wonder if we will ever find the love we long for, or if we are missing out on something that others seem to have. In these moments, it is easy to become discouraged and to lose hope.

However, the Bible encourages us to see waiting not as a burden, but as an opportunity for growth and transformation. In Isaiah 40:31, we read, *"But they who wait for the Lord shall renew their strength; they shall mount up with wings like eagles; they shall run and not be weary; they shall walk and not faint."* Waiting on the Lord is a time of renewal and strengthening, as we learn to rely on His strength and to trust in His timing.

2. The Role of Hope in Waiting: Hope is what sustains us during the waiting period. It is the confident assurance that God is at work, even when we cannot see the immediate results. Hope allows us to endure the challenges of waiting with patience and perseverance, knowing that God's promises are sure.

In Romans 8:28, Paul reminds us that *"we know that for those who love God all things work together for good, for those who are called according to his purpose."* This verse is a powerful reminder that God is working all things together for our good, even in the waiting. Our hope is not in the circumstances themselves, but in the God who is sovereign over all circumstances.

Hope also gives us the courage to continue pursuing love, even when the path is uncertain. It allows us to remain open to the possibilities that God may bring into our lives, and to trust that His plans for us are good. As we place our hope in God's promises, we can move forward with confidence, knowing that He is leading us towards a future filled with love and fulfillment.

3. The Transformative Power of Hope: Hope has the power to transform our perspective and our lives. When we hold onto hope in the midst of waiting, we begin to see our circumstances through the lens of God's promises, rather than through the lens of our own fears or doubts.

Hope enables us to approach the waiting period with a sense of purpose and expectation, rather than with a sense of despair or resignation. It shifts our focus from what we lack to what God is doing in our lives, and it opens our hearts to the possibility of new beginnings.

Moreover, hope produces in us the fruit of joy and peace, even in the midst of uncertainty. As Paul writes in Romans 15:13, the God of hope fills us with joy and peace as we believe in His promises. This joy and peace are not dependent on our circumstances; they are gifts from God that sustain us through the waiting and that prepare us for the fulfillment of His promises.

God's Promises and the Fulfillment of Love

THE HOPE THAT SUSTAINS us while waiting for love is rooted in the promises of God. These promises provide a foundation for our hope, assuring us that God's plans for us are good and that He is faithful to fulfill His word. As we reflect on God's promises, we can find strength, courage, and peace in the waiting.

1. The Promise of God's Timing: One of the most comforting promises in Scripture is the assurance that God's timing is perfect. In Ecclesiastes 3:11, we read, *"He has made everything beautiful in its time."* This verse reminds us that God's timing is not arbitrary; it is purposeful and perfect.

When it comes to love, God's timing may not always align with our own desires or expectations. We may find ourselves waiting longer than we anticipated, or we may experience detours and setbacks along the way. However, the promise of God's timing assures us that He is orchestrating the events of our lives according to His perfect plan.

As we place our hope in God's timing, we can trust that He is preparing us for the love that He has in store for us. This preparation may involve personal growth, healing, or the development of certain qualities that will make us better partners in the future. Whatever the process, we can be confident that God's timing is working for our ultimate good.

2. The Promise of God's Guidance: Another important promise is the assurance of God's guidance in our lives. In Proverbs 3:5-6, we are instructed to *"Trust in the Lord with all your heart, and do not lean on your own understanding. In all your ways acknowledge him, and he will make straight your paths."* This promise of guidance is a source of hope and comfort, especially in times of uncertainty.

As we wait for love, we can trust that God is leading us and guiding our steps. This guidance may come in the form of opportunities, relationships, or circumstances that align with His will for our lives. It may also involve closing doors or redirecting our paths in ways that we did not expect.

Whatever the form of God's guidance, we can be confident that He is leading us towards the fulfillment of His promises. Our hope is not in our own ability to navigate the complexities of life; it is in the God who is sovereign over all things and who is faithfully guiding us according to His purposes.

3. The Promise of God's Presence: One of the most precious promises in Scripture is the assurance of God's presence with us at all times. In Matthew 28:20, Jesus promises His disciples, *"And behold, I am with you always, to the end of the age."* This promise of God's constant presence is a source of hope and strength, especially in times of waiting.

As we wait for love, we can find comfort in the knowledge that we are never alone. God is with us, walking alongside us, and carrying us through the challenges and uncertainties of life. His presence is a reminder that we are loved, valued, and cherished, even when we are waiting for human love to be fulfilled.

The promise of God's presence also gives us the courage to wait with hope, knowing that He is with us every step of the way. His presence is a source of strength, peace, and encouragement, enabling us to endure the waiting period with grace and patience.

4. The Promise of God's Provision: Finally, we have the promise of God's provision in our lives. In Philippians 4:19, Paul writes, *"And my God will supply every need of yours according to his riches in glory in Christ Jesus."* This promise of provision assures us that God will meet our needs, both now and in the future.

When it comes to love, this promise of provision is a source of hope and reassurance. We can trust that God knows our needs and that He is working to provide for us in ways that we may not even be aware of. This provision may come in the form of a loving relationship, a supportive community, or the fulfillment of other desires and dreams.

Whatever the form of God's provision, we can be confident that He is faithful to meet our needs according to His riches in glory. Our hope is not in our own ability to provide for ourselves; it is in the God who is the ultimate provider and who delights in giving good gifts to His children.

The Challenges of Maintaining Hope

WHILE HOPE IS A POWERFUL and sustaining force, it is not without its challenges. Maintaining hope in the midst of waiting can be difficult, especially when faced with disappointments, delays, or uncertainties. However, it is precisely in these moments of challenge that hope becomes most vital.

1. The Challenge of Discouragement: One of the greatest challenges to maintaining hope is the experience of discouragement. When we face setbacks, delays, or disappointments, it is easy to become discouraged and to lose sight of the hope that we have in God's promises.

In these moments, it is important to remember that discouragement is a natural part of the human experience, but it does not have to define our outlook or our faith. The Bible offers numerous examples of individuals who faced discouragement yet held onto hope in God's promises.

One such example is the story of Abraham and Sarah, who waited many years for the fulfillment of God's promise of a child. Despite the challenges and setbacks they faced, they continued to hope in God's promise, and in time, they saw that promise fulfilled in the birth of their son Isaac.

In Romans 4:18-21, Paul reflects on Abraham's hope: *"In hope he believed against hope, that he should become the father of many nations, as he had been told, 'So shall your offspring be.' He did not weaken in faith when he considered his own body, which was as good as dead (since he was about a hundred years old), or when he considered the barrenness of Sarah's womb. No unbelief made him waver concerning the promise of God, but he grew strong in his faith as he gave glory to God, fully convinced that God was able to do what he had promised."*

Like Abraham, we are called to hold onto hope, even in the face of discouragement. Our hope is not based on our circumstances or our own abilities; it is based on the character and promises of God, who is faithful and able to fulfill His word.

2. The Challenge of Doubt: Another significant challenge to maintaining hope is the experience of doubt. Doubt can arise when we question whether God's promises will really come to pass, or when we struggle to see how God is at work in our lives.

In these moments of doubt, it is important to remember that doubt is not the opposite of faith; it is a part of the faith journey. The Bible is filled with stories of individuals who experienced doubt yet continued to trust in God's promises.

One such example is the story of Thomas, one of Jesus' disciples, who struggled with doubt after the resurrection. In John 20:24-29, we read about how Jesus gently addressed Thomas's doubts, inviting him to see and touch the wounds in His hands and side. Thomas's response was one of faith and worship, as he declared, *"My Lord and my God!"*

Jesus's response to Thomas's doubt reminds us that God is not afraid of our doubts. He meets us in our doubts and invites us to trust in His promises. As we bring our doubts to God in prayer and seek His guidance, we can find renewed hope and confidence in His faithfulness.

3. The Challenge of Patience: Maintaining hope also requires patience, a virtue that can be difficult to cultivate, especially in a culture that values instant gratification and quick results. Patience involves waiting for God's timing and trusting that His plans for us are good, even when we do not see immediate results.

In James 5:7-8, we are encouraged to *"Be patient, therefore, brothers, until the coming of the Lord. See how the farmer waits for the precious fruit of the earth, being patient about it, until it receives the early and the late rains. You also, be patient. Establish your hearts, for the coming of the Lord is at hand."*

This passage reminds us that patience is a key aspect of hope. Just as the farmer waits for the fruit of the earth, we are called to wait patiently for the fulfillment of God's promises. This patience is not passive; it is an active expression of trust and hope, as we continue to seek God's will and to live in obedience to His word.

4. The Challenge of Surrender: Finally, maintaining hope requires surrender—surrendering our own plans, desires, and timelines to God, and trusting that His plans for us are better than anything we could imagine. Surrender involves letting go of control and allowing God to lead us according to His will.

In Proverbs 16:9, we are reminded that *"The heart of man plans his way, but the Lord establishes his steps."* This verse highlights the tension between our own plans and God's sovereignty. While it is natural for us to make plans and to have desires, we are ultimately called to surrender those plans to God, trusting that He will establish our steps according to His perfect will.

Surrender is not easy, especially when it involves letting go of something we deeply desire. However, it is through surrender that we find true freedom and peace, as we place our hope in God's promises rather than in our own efforts or understanding.

The Rewards of Hope

DESPITE THE CHALLENGES of maintaining hope, the rewards are abundant and transformative. Hope brings with it a deep sense of joy, peace, and fulfillment, as we place our trust in God's promises and His faithfulness.

1. The Joy of Expectation: One of the most significant rewards of hope is the joy that comes from living in expectation of God's promises. This joy is not dependent on our circumstances; it is a deep and abiding sense of well-being that comes from knowing that God is at work in our lives.

In Romans 12:12, Paul encourages believers to *"Rejoice in hope, be patient in tribulation, be constant in prayer."* This exhortation reminds us that joy and hope are closely connected. As we place our hope in God's promises, we experience the joy of expectation, knowing that God is faithful and that His plans for us are good.

This joy is a powerful testimony to the world, as it reflects the transformative power of God's grace and love in our lives. It is a joy that cannot be shaken by circumstances or challenges, as it is rooted in the unchanging character of God.

2. The Peace of Trust: Another significant reward of hope is the peace that comes from trusting in God's promises. This peace is not merely the absence of conflict or anxiety; it is a deep sense of calm and assurance that comes from knowing that God is in control.

In Philippians 4:6-7, Paul writes, *"Do not be anxious about anything, but in everything by prayer and supplication with thanksgiving let your requests be made known to God. And the peace of God, which surpasses all understanding, will guard your hearts and your minds in Christ Jesus."*

This promise of peace is a source of hope and comfort, especially in times of uncertainty or difficulty. As we place our hope in God's promises and bring our concerns to Him in prayer, we experience the peace of God that guards our hearts and minds, allowing us to navigate the challenges of life with confidence and serenity.

3. The Fulfillment of God's Promises: Ultimately, the greatest reward of hope is the fulfillment of God's promises in our lives. While we may not always see the immediate results of our hope, we can trust that God is faithful and that His promises will come to pass.

In Hebrews 10:23, we are encouraged to "Hold fast the confession of our hope without wavering, for he who promised is faithful." This verse reminds us that our hope is not in vain; it is based on the character and faithfulness of God, who is true to His word.

As we hold onto hope and trust in God's promises, we will eventually see those promises fulfilled in our lives. Whether it be in the form of a loving relationship, the realization of a dream, or the deepening of our relationship with God, the fulfillment of God's promises brings with it a deep sense of joy, satisfaction, and fulfillment.

4. The Growth of Faith: Finally, hope leads to the growth of our faith. As we place our hope in God's promises and trust in His timing, our faith is strengthened and deepened. This growth of faith is one of the most significant rewards of hope, as it draws us closer to God and transforms our lives.

In James 1:2-4, we are encouraged to "Count it all joy, my brothers, when you meet trials of various kinds, for you know that the testing of your faith produces steadfastness. And let steadfastness have its full effect, that you may be perfect and complete, lacking in nothing."

This passage reminds us that the testing of our faith, including the challenges of waiting and maintaining hope, leads to spiritual growth and maturity. As we persevere in hope, we become more steadfast, more complete, and more aligned with God's will for our lives.

Practical Steps for Cultivating Hope

CULTIVATING HOPE IN our lives requires intentionality, effort, and a deep reliance on God's strength and guidance. Here are some practical steps to help you cultivate and maintain hope in your journey of waiting for love:

1. Ground Your Hope in God's Word: Begin by grounding your hope in the promises of God's Word. Spend time in Scripture, reflecting on the promises that God has made and how they apply to your life. Allow the truths of God's Word to strengthen your hope and to remind you of His faithfulness.

2. Pray for the Holy Spirit's Help: Ask the Holy Spirit to fill you with hope, joy, and peace as you trust in God's promises. The Holy Spirit is

the source of our hope, and He empowers us to hold onto hope even in difficult circumstances. Be constant in prayer, bringing your hopes, concerns, and desires before God.

3. Surround Yourself with Encouragement: Surround yourself with a community of believers who can encourage you and support you in your journey of hope. Whether through a small group, a mentor, or close friends, having a support system can help you to maintain hope and to stay focused on God's promises.

4. Practice Gratitude: Cultivate a heart of gratitude by regularly giving thanks to God for the blessings in your life. Gratitude shifts our focus from what we lack to what God has already provided, and it helps to sustain our hope in His continued faithfulness.

5. Embrace the Waiting: Rather than viewing the waiting period as a burden, embrace it as an opportunity for growth and transformation. Trust that God is at work in your life, preparing you for the love and fulfillment that He has in store for you. Allow the waiting to deepen your faith and to draw you closer to God.

6. Surrender Your Desires to God: Finally, practice surrender by entrusting your desires, plans, and timelines to God. Trust that His plans for you are good, and that He will fulfill His promises in His perfect timing. Surrendering to God brings freedom and peace, as you place your hope in His sovereign will.

Conclusion: The Hope that Sustains Us

HOPE IS A POWERFUL and sustaining force that enables us to navigate the challenges of life with joy, peace, and confidence. It is rooted in the promises of God and is sustained by the power of the Holy Spirit. As we place our hope in God's promises, we can endure the waiting periods of life with patience and perseverance, knowing that God is faithful and that His plans for us are good.

Romans 15:13 reminds us that the God of hope fills us with all joy and peace in believing, so that by the power of the Holy Spirit we may abound in hope. This hope is not dependent on our circumstances; it is grounded in the unchanging character of God, who is faithful to fulfill His word.

As you navigate the journey of waiting for love, may you be encouraged to place your hope in God's promises. Ground your hope in His Word, pray for the Holy Spirit's help, and embrace the waiting period as an opportunity for growth and transformation. Trust that God's plans for you are good, and that He is leading you towards a future filled with love, fulfillment, and joy.

May your hope in God's promises sustain you, strengthen you, and bring you peace as you wait for the love that He has in store for you. And may you experience the profound joy and fulfillment that come from living in the light of God's hope, trusting in His faithfulness, and embracing the future that He has prepared for you.

Chapter 13: Finding Contentment in Singleness

Theological **Reflection:** Reflect on finding contentment in singleness while waiting for love. Philippians 4:11-13 offers a perspective on being content in any situation, including waiting for the right partner.

Introduction: The Journey of Singleness

SINGLENESS IS A SEASON that many people experience at various points in their lives, and it can evoke a wide range of emotions. For some, singleness is a time of freedom, growth, and self-discovery. For others, it can be marked by loneliness, frustration, and a deep longing for companionship. In a culture that often places a high value on romantic relationships and marriage, it can be challenging to find contentment and fulfillment in singleness.

However, the Bible offers a different perspective on singleness—one that invites us to see this season as a gift rather than a burden. The Apostle Paul, in his letter to the Philippians, speaks about the secret of contentment, regardless of circumstances. In Philippians 4:11-13, Paul writes, *"I have learned in whatever situation I am to be content. I know how to be brought low, and I know how to abound. In any and every circumstance, I have learned the secret of facing plenty and hunger, abundance and need. I can do all things through him who strengthens me."*

These verses remind us that contentment is not dependent on our external circumstances—whether we are single or in a relationship, experiencing abundance or lack. True contentment comes from a deep, abiding relationship with Christ, who strengthens us and provides for all our needs.

In this chapter, we will explore the concept of contentment in singleness, reflecting on how to find joy, peace, and fulfillment in this season while waiting for love. We will consider the theological significance of contentment, the challenges of embracing singleness, and the ways in which God can use this season for growth and transformation. Drawing from Philippians 4:11-13, we will discover how to cultivate a heart of contentment that is rooted in Christ, enabling us to thrive in singleness and beyond.

The Theological Foundation of Contentment

CONTENTMENT IS A CENTRAL theme in Christian theology, closely tied to the concepts of trust, gratitude, and reliance on God. The Bible teaches that contentment is not about settling for less or denying our desires; rather, it is about finding satisfaction and peace in God, regardless of our circumstances.

1. Contentment as a Gift from God: Contentment is not something that we can manufacture on our own; it is a gift from God. In 1 Timothy 6:6, Paul writes, *"But godliness with contentment is great gain."* This verse highlights the connection between godliness—living in a way that honors God—and contentment. When we pursue a life of godliness, seeking to align our hearts and actions with God's will, contentment naturally follows.

This contentment is a deep, abiding sense of peace and satisfaction that comes from knowing and trusting in God's provision. It is rooted in the belief that God is sovereign and that He is working all things together for our good. When we embrace this truth, we are able to find contentment in any situation, including singleness, because we trust that God's plans for us are good.

2. The Secret of Contentment in Christ: In Philippians 4:11-13, Paul speaks about learning the secret of contentment. This secret is not found in our circumstances—whether we have plenty or are in need—but in our relationship with Christ. Paul writes, *"I can do all things through him who strengthens me."* This verse is often quoted in the context of achieving great things, but its true meaning is about finding strength and contentment in Christ, regardless of our external situation.

Paul's contentment was not dependent on whether he was hungry or well-fed, whether he was in abundance or in need. His contentment was rooted in his relationship with Christ, who provided him with the strength to endure all circumstances. This same strength is available to us today, enabling us to find contentment in singleness and in all areas of life.

3. Trusting in God's Provision: Contentment is closely tied to trust in God's provision. When we trust that God knows our needs and is faithful to provide for them, we can find peace and satisfaction in the present moment, rather than constantly longing for something more. In Matthew 6:31-33, Jesus encourages His followers not to worry about their needs, saying, *"Therefore do not be anxious, saying, 'What shall we eat?' or 'What shall we drink?' or 'What shall we wear?' For the Gentiles seek after all these things, and your heavenly Father knows that you need them all. But seek first the kingdom of God and his righteousness, and all these things will be added to you."*

This passage reminds us that God is aware of our needs, including our desire for love and companionship, and that He is faithful to provide for us in His perfect timing. When we seek God's kingdom first, trusting in His provision, we can find contentment in the present moment, knowing that God is working all things together for our good.

Embracing Singleness as a Season of Growth

SINGLENESS, LIKE ANY other season of life, presents unique opportunities for growth, self-discovery, and spiritual development. While it is natural to desire a loving relationship, it is also important to recognize the value and potential of the season of singleness.

1. Singleness as a Gift: In 1 Corinthians 7, Paul speaks about singleness as a gift. He writes, *"I wish that all were as I myself am. But each has his own gift from God, one of one kind and one of another"* (1 Corinthians 7:7). Paul, who was single, viewed his singleness as a gift that allowed him to serve God without distraction. He saw the value in being fully devoted to the work of the Lord, unencumbered by the responsibilities of marriage.

While not everyone is called to lifelong singleness, this passage encourages us to view singleness as a season with its own unique gifts and opportunities. Rather than seeing singleness as a time of waiting or lack, we can embrace it as a time to fully invest in our relationship with God, to pursue our passions and callings, and to grow as individuals.

2. Personal Growth and Development: Singleness is an ideal time for personal growth and development. Without the demands of a romantic relationship, we have the freedom and space to focus on our own well-being, to develop our talents and skills, and to pursue our goals and dreams.

This season can be a time of self-discovery, as we explore our interests, values, and identity. It is an opportunity to become more self-aware, to understand our strengths and weaknesses, and to grow in confidence and maturity. As we invest in our personal growth, we are not only preparing ourselves for a potential future relationship but also enriching our lives in the present.

3. Spiritual Growth and Intimacy with God: Perhaps the most significant opportunity in singleness is the chance to deepen our relationship with God. In 1 Corinthians 7:32-35, Paul speaks about the advantages of singleness in terms of devotion to the Lord: *"I want you to be free from anxieties. The unmarried man is anxious about the things of the Lord, how to please the Lord. But the married man is anxious about worldly things, how to please his wife, and his interests are divided. And the unmarried or betrothed woman is anxious about the things of the Lord, how to be holy in body and spirit."*

Singleness provides us with the time and space to focus on our spiritual growth, to spend time in prayer and Scripture, and to cultivate a deep and intimate relationship with God. This season can be a time of spiritual renewal, where we learn to rely on God's strength, to seek His guidance, and to trust in His plans for our lives.

4. Building Meaningful Relationships: Singleness also provides an opportunity to build meaningful relationships outside of a romantic context. Friendships, family relationships, and community connections are all vital aspects of a fulfilling life. During this season, we can invest in these relationships, building strong bonds of love, support, and mutual encouragement.

These relationships can provide a sense of belonging and connection, reminding us that we are not alone, even in our singleness. They also help us to develop the qualities that are essential for any healthy relationship, such as communication, empathy, and selflessness.

Overcoming the Challenges of Singleness

WHILE SINGLENESS OFFERS many opportunities for growth and fulfillment, it is not without its challenges. Feelings of loneliness, societal pressures, and the longing for companionship can all make it difficult to find contentment in this season. However, these challenges can also be opportunities for deepening our trust in God and for developing resilience and strength.

1. Loneliness and the Desire for Companionship: One of the most common challenges of singleness is the experience of loneliness and the deep desire for companionship. It is natural to long for connection and intimacy, and these desires are not wrong in themselves. However, when they become the focus of our thoughts and emotions, they can lead to discontentment and frustration.

In these moments, it is important to remember that our ultimate source of fulfillment and connection is found in God. Psalm 73:25-26 reminds us, *"Whom have I in heaven but you? And there is nothing on earth that I desire besides you. My flesh and my heart may fail, but God is the strength of my heart and my portion forever."*

This passage encourages us to turn to God in our moments of loneliness, trusting that He is our true source of companionship and strength. As we cultivate a deeper relationship with God, we can find that our loneliness is eased, and our hearts are filled with His love and presence.

2. Societal Pressures and Expectations: Another challenge of singleness is the societal pressure to be in a relationship or to get married. In many cultures, there is an expectation that individuals should be in a romantic relationship by a certain age, and those who are not may feel judged, pitied, or even marginalized.

These societal pressures can create feelings of inadequacy or failure, leading to a sense of discontentment in singleness. However, it is important to remember that our worth and identity are not determined by our relationship status but by our relationship with Christ. In Galatians 2:20, Paul writes, *"I have been crucified with Christ. It is no longer I who live, but Christ who lives in me. And the life I now live in the flesh I live by faith in the Son of God, who loved me and gave himself for me."*

This verse reminds us that our identity is found in Christ, not in the expectations or opinions of others. As we focus on our relationship with Christ, we can find the confidence and freedom to live according to His will, rather than conforming to societal pressures.

3. The Challenge of Comparison: In today's world of social media and constant connectivity, it is easy to fall into the trap of comparison. We may see others who are in relationships, getting married, or starting families, and we may begin to compare our lives to theirs. This comparison can lead to feelings of envy, inadequacy, and discontentment.

However, the Bible warns us against the dangers of comparison. In 2 Corinthians 10:12, Paul writes, *"Not that we dare to classify or compare ourselves with some of those who are commending themselves. But when they measure themselves by one another and compare themselves with one another, they are without understanding."*

This verse reminds us that comparison is unwise and unhelpful. Instead of focusing on what others have, we are called to focus on what God has given us and to be grateful for His blessings. As we cultivate a heart of gratitude, we can find contentment in our own journey, trusting that God's plans for us are unique and good.

4. The Challenge of Patience: Singleness often requires patience, especially for those who desire to be in a relationship or to get married. Waiting for the right person, the right time, or the fulfillment of God's plans can be challenging, and it is easy to become impatient or discouraged.

In these moments, it is important to remember the value of patience and trust in God's timing. In Psalm 27:14, we are encouraged to *"Wait for the Lord; be strong, and let your heart take courage; wait for the Lord!"* This verse reminds us that waiting is not a passive activity but an active expression of trust and courage.

As we wait for God's timing, we can focus on the present moment, finding joy and contentment in the here and now. We can trust that God is at work, preparing us for the future He has in store, and that His timing is perfect.

The Rewards of Contentment in Singleness

FINDING CONTENTMENT in singleness brings with it many rewards, both in our relationship with God and in our overall well-being. Contentment allows us to live fully in the present moment, to experience joy and peace, and to grow in our faith and character.

1. The Joy of Living in the Present: One of the greatest rewards of contentment is the ability to live fully in the present moment. When we are content, we are not constantly longing for the future or dwelling on what we lack; instead, we are able to appreciate the blessings and opportunities of the present.

In Ecclesiastes 3:12-13, the writer reflects on the value of enjoying life's blessings in the present: *"I perceived that there is nothing better for them than to be joyful and to do good as long as they live; also that everyone should eat and drink and take pleasure in all his toil—this is God's gift to man."*

This passage encourages us to find joy in the simple pleasures of life, to do good, and to take pleasure in our work and activities. As we embrace the present moment, we can experience the fullness of life that God has given us, finding contentment and joy in the here and now.

2. The Peace of Trusting in God's Plan: Contentment also brings with it a deep sense of peace, as we trust in God's plan for our lives. This peace is not dependent on our circumstances; it is rooted in our relationship with Christ and our confidence in His sovereignty.

In Isaiah 26:3, we read, *"You keep him in perfect peace whose mind is stayed on you, because he trusts in you."* This verse reminds us that peace comes from keeping our focus on God and trusting in His plan for our lives. As we place our trust in God, we can experience a peace that surpasses all understanding, even in the midst of singleness.

3. The Growth of Faith and Character: Singleness is a season of growth, both in our faith and in our character. As we learn to find contentment in Christ, we develop qualities such as patience, perseverance, humility, and

resilience. These qualities are essential for any healthy relationship and are valuable in all areas of life.

In James 1:2-4, we are encouraged to *"Count it all joy, my brothers, when you meet trials of various kinds, for you know that the testing of your faith produces steadfastness. And let steadfastness have its full effect, that you may be perfect and complete, lacking in nothing."*

This passage reminds us that trials, including the challenges of singleness, are opportunities for growth. As we persevere in our faith and find contentment in Christ, we become more complete and mature, lacking in nothing.

4. The Freedom to Pursue God's Calling: Contentment in singleness also provides the freedom to pursue God's calling in our lives without distraction. When we are content, we are not weighed down by the pressure to find a relationship or to conform to societal expectations. Instead, we are free to focus on what God has called us to do, whether in our work, ministry, or personal pursuits.

In Ephesians 2:10, Paul writes, *"For we are his workmanship, created in Christ Jesus for good works, which God prepared beforehand, that we should walk in them."* This verse reminds us that we are uniquely created for a purpose, and that God has prepared good works for us to do. As we find contentment in singleness, we can fully embrace our calling and live out the purpose that God has for our lives.

Practical Steps for Finding Contentment in Singleness

FINDING CONTENTMENT in singleness requires intentionality, effort, and a deep reliance on God's strength and guidance. Here are some practical steps to help you cultivate contentment in this season:

1. Focus on Your Relationship with Christ: The foundation of contentment is a deep, abiding relationship with Christ. Spend time in prayer, Scripture, and worship, cultivating your relationship with God. As you grow closer to Christ, you will find that He is your source of strength, peace, and contentment.

2. Practice Gratitude: Cultivate a heart of gratitude by regularly giving thanks to God for the blessings in your life. Gratitude shifts our focus from

what we lack to what we have, helping us to find contentment in the present moment. Keep a gratitude journal, listing the things you are thankful for each day.

3. Invest in Personal Growth: Use this season of singleness to invest in your personal growth and development. Pursue your passions, develop your talents, and set goals for yourself. As you focus on becoming the best version of yourself, you will find fulfillment and contentment in your own journey.

4. Build Meaningful Relationships: Invest in your friendships, family relationships, and community connections. These relationships provide a sense of belonging and support, reminding you that you are not alone. Surround yourself with people who encourage you and help you grow.

5. Trust in God's Timing: Trust that God's timing is perfect, and that He is working all things together for your good. Be patient and surrender your desires to God, trusting that He knows what is best for you. Focus on the present moment, and trust that God's plans for your future are good.

6. Live Fully in the Present: Embrace the present moment, finding joy and contentment in the here and now. Focus on what God is doing in your life today, rather than constantly longing for the future. Find pleasure in the simple things, and live each day with purpose and gratitude.

Conclusion: The Gift of Contentment in Singleness

CONTENTMENT IN SINGLENESS is not about settling for less or denying our desires; it is about finding peace, joy, and fulfillment in Christ, regardless of our circumstances. Philippians 4:11-13 reminds us that contentment is not dependent on whether we are single or in a relationship; it is rooted in our relationship with Christ, who strengthens us and provides for all our needs.

As you navigate the season of singleness, may you be encouraged to find contentment in Christ, trusting that His plans for you are good. Embrace this season as a time of growth, self-discovery, and spiritual renewal, and focus on the present moment, finding joy in the here and now.

May you experience the profound peace and fulfillment that come from living fully in the present, trusting in God's provision, and finding contentment in His love. And may you be reminded that your worth and identity are not determined by your relationship status, but by your relationship with Christ, who loves you and has a purpose for your life.

As you continue on your journey, may you find that contentment in singleness is not just a possibility, but a gift—one that allows you to live with joy, purpose, and freedom, knowing that you are exactly where God wants you to be.

Chapter 14: The Joy of Love Fulfilled

Theological Reflection: Explore the joy that comes when love is finally fulfilled. Use Psalm 37:4 to discuss the delight in receiving the desires of the heart when they align with God's will.

Introduction: The Longing for Fulfillment

THE DESIRE FOR LOVE is one of the most profound and universal longings of the human heart. From the earliest stories of humanity, love has been portrayed as a powerful force that can inspire greatness, bring deep joy, and create lasting bonds. The Bible itself is full of stories about love—between God and humanity, between friends, between families, and between romantic partners. In these stories, love is often depicted as both a source of profound happiness and a driving force behind many of the actions and decisions people make.

For those who have experienced the season of waiting, the fulfillment of love can bring immense joy and satisfaction. The journey to this point may have been filled with challenges, uncertainties, and long periods of waiting, but the moment when love is finally realized can feel like a beautiful culmination of all those experiences. It's a moment when the desires of the heart align with God's will, and the result is a profound sense of joy and peace.

Psalm 37:4 offers a beautiful promise that speaks to this experience: *"Delight yourself in the Lord, and he will give you the desires of your heart."* This verse reminds us that when our desires are aligned with God's will—when we delight in Him above all else—He fulfills those desires in ways that are truly satisfying and life-giving.

In this chapter, we will explore the joy that comes when love is finally fulfilled. We will reflect on the theological significance of love's fulfillment, the journey of waiting and trusting in God's timing, and the ways in which God delights in giving us the desires of our hearts. Drawing from Psalm 37:4, we will consider how the fulfillment of love brings not only personal happiness but also a deeper connection with God and a greater understanding of His goodness and faithfulness.

The Theological Foundation of Fulfilled Love

THE CONCEPT OF FULFILLED love is deeply rooted in the character of God and His relationship with humanity. Throughout the Bible, God is depicted as a loving and faithful Father who delights in giving good gifts to His children. This includes the fulfillment of our deepest desires, particularly when those desires align with His will and purposes.

1. God's Love as the Source of All Fulfillment: At the heart of all true love is God, who is love itself. 1 John 4:8 tells us that *"God is love,"* meaning that love is not just something God does; it is who He is. Because God is love, all genuine love originates from Him and is a reflection of His character.

When we experience the fulfillment of love in our lives—whether it be in the form of a romantic relationship, a deep friendship, or the love of family—it is ultimately a reflection of God's love for us. This fulfillment is a reminder that God is the source of all love and that He delights in blessing His children with the gift of love.

2. The Joy of God's Presence: The joy that comes with the fulfillment of love is not just about the relationship itself; it is also about experiencing the presence of God in a new and profound way. In Psalm 16:11, David writes, *"You make known to me the path of life; in your presence there is fullness of joy; at your right hand are pleasures forevermore."*

This verse reminds us that true joy is found in the presence of God, and that the fulfillment of our desires is deeply connected to our relationship with Him. When our love is fulfilled, it is not just a temporal joy; it is an experience of God's presence and His goodness in our lives.

3. The Alignment of Desires with God's Will: Psalm 37:4 offers a powerful promise: *"Delight yourself in the Lord, and he will give you the desires of your

heart."* This verse highlights the importance of aligning our desires with God's will. When we delight in the Lord—when we seek His will, His presence, and His guidance above all else—our desires become aligned with His desires for us.

This alignment is key to experiencing the joy of fulfilled love. When our desires are in harmony with God's will, the fulfillment of those desires brings not just happiness but also a deep sense of peace and satisfaction, knowing that we are walking in God's plan for our lives.

4. God's Faithfulness in Fulfilling Promises: The fulfillment of love is also a testament to God's faithfulness. Throughout the Bible, God is portrayed as a faithful covenant-keeper, who fulfills His promises to His people. In Lamentations 3:22-23, we read, *"The steadfast love of the Lord never ceases; his mercies never come to an end; they are new every morning; great is your faithfulness."*

When we experience the fulfillment of love, it is a reminder of God's faithfulness to His promises. It is an opportunity to reflect on the ways in which God has been faithful in our lives, even in the times of waiting and uncertainty. This fulfillment strengthens our faith and deepens our trust in God's goodness and sovereignty.

The Journey of Waiting and Trusting in God's Timing

THE JOURNEY TO THE fulfillment of love is often marked by periods of waiting, uncertainty, and trust in God's timing. These seasons of waiting can be challenging, but they are also opportunities for growth, transformation, and deeper reliance on God.

1. The Purpose of Waiting: Waiting is a common theme in the Bible, and it is often portrayed as a time of preparation, testing, and refinement. In Isaiah 40:31, we read, *"But they who wait for the Lord shall renew their strength; they shall mount up with wings like eagles; they shall run and not be weary; they shall walk and not faint."* This verse reminds us that waiting on the Lord is not passive; it is an active process of renewal and strengthening.

In the context of love, waiting is an opportunity to grow in our relationship with God, to develop patience and perseverance, and to prepare ourselves for the fulfillment of the desires He has placed in our hearts. It is a time to trust in God's wisdom and timing, knowing that He is at work even when we cannot see the immediate results.

2. Trusting in God's Sovereignty: Trusting in God's timing is a key aspect of the journey to fulfilled love. Proverbs 3:5-6 encourages us to *"Trust in the Lord with all your heart, and do not lean on your own understanding. In all your ways acknowledge him, and he will make straight your paths."* This passage reminds us that our understanding is limited, but God's wisdom is perfect.

When we trust in God's sovereignty, we can rest in the assurance that His timing is always right. Even when the waiting seems long or the path seems unclear, we can trust that God is orchestrating the events of our lives according to His perfect plan. This trust allows us to wait with hope, knowing that God's timing is working for our good and His glory.

3. The Role of Faith in Waiting: Faith is essential in the journey of waiting for love to be fulfilled. Hebrews 11:1 defines faith as *"the assurance of things hoped for, the conviction of things not seen."* This assurance and conviction enable us to hold onto God's promises, even when the fulfillment is not yet visible.

In the context of love, faith allows us to believe that God has a good plan for our lives, even when we are in a season of waiting. It gives us the strength to continue seeking God's will, to remain faithful in our relationship with Him, and to trust that He will fulfill the desires of our hearts in His perfect timing.

4. The Transformation of Waiting: Waiting is not just about passing the time until our desires are fulfilled; it is about transformation. Romans 5:3-5 speaks to the transformative power of waiting and endurance: *"Not only that, but we rejoice in our sufferings, knowing that suffering produces endurance, and endurance produces character, and character produces hope, and hope does not put us to shame, because God's love has been poured into our hearts through the Holy Spirit who has been given to us."*

As we wait for love to be fulfilled, we are being transformed. Our character is being shaped, our faith is being strengthened, and our hope is being deepened. This transformation prepares us to receive the fulfillment of love with gratitude and joy, knowing that it is the result of God's work in our lives.

The Joy of Love Fulfilled

THE MOMENT WHEN LOVE is finally fulfilled is a time of great joy and celebration. It is a moment when the desires of the heart are realized, and the waiting and trusting in God's timing come to fruition. This joy is not just about the fulfillment of a desire; it is about experiencing the goodness, faithfulness, and love of God in a profound and personal way.

1. The Experience of God's Goodness: The fulfillment of love is a tangible experience of God's goodness. In Psalm 34:8, we are invited to *"Taste and see that the Lord is good; blessed is the one who takes refuge in him."* This verse invites us to experience God's goodness in a personal and intimate way.

When love is fulfilled, we taste and see God's goodness in our lives. We experience the joy of receiving the desires of our hearts, and we are reminded of God's kindness, generosity, and care for us. This experience of God's goodness deepens our relationship with Him and fills our hearts with gratitude and praise.

2. The Fulfillment of God's Promises: The joy of fulfilled love is also a celebration of the fulfillment of God's promises. In 2 Corinthians 1:20, Paul writes, *"For all the promises of God find their Yes in him. That is why it is through him that we utter our Amen to God for his glory."* This verse reminds us that every promise of God is fulfilled in Christ.

When love is fulfilled, we see the evidence of God's promises coming to pass in our lives. This fulfillment strengthens our faith and reminds us that God is faithful to His word. It is an opportunity to reflect on the journey we have been on and to give thanks for the ways in which God has been faithful to us.

3. The Joy of Unity and Connection: Love's fulfillment brings with it the joy of unity and connection. In Genesis 2:24, we read, *"Therefore a man shall leave his father and his mother and hold fast to his wife, and they shall become one flesh."* This verse speaks to the deep connection and unity that is experienced in a loving relationship.

When love is fulfilled, we experience the joy of being united with another person in a deep and meaningful way. This unity is not just physical; it is emotional, spiritual, and relational. It is a reflection of the unity that we have with God through Christ, and it brings a deep sense of fulfillment and satisfaction.

4. The Impact of Fulfilled Love on Others: The joy of fulfilled love is not just for the individuals involved; it has a ripple effect on those around them. In John 15:11, Jesus says, *"These things I have spoken to you, that my joy may be in you, and that your joy may be full."* This verse reminds us that the joy of Christ in us is meant to be shared and to bring joy to others.

When love is fulfilled, it brings joy to the community, to family and friends, and to all those who have been part of the journey. It is a testimony to God's goodness and faithfulness, and it serves as an encouragement to others who are waiting for their own desires to be fulfilled. The joy of fulfilled love is a gift that keeps on giving, spreading happiness and hope to those around us.

Delighting in the Lord and Receiving the Desires of the Heart

PSALM 37:4 OFFERS A beautiful promise that is central to the experience of fulfilled love: *"Delight yourself in the Lord, and he will give you the desires of your heart."* This verse invites us to consider the relationship between our desires and our delight in the Lord.

1. The Meaning of Delighting in the Lord: To delight in the Lord means to take joy and pleasure in who God is and in our relationship with Him. It involves seeking His presence, His will, and His guidance in all aspects of our lives. When we delight in the Lord, we find our greatest satisfaction in knowing Him and in living according to His purposes.

Delighting in the Lord is not just about doing religious activities; it is about cultivating a deep, personal relationship with God. It is about prioritizing our relationship with Him above all else and finding our identity, purpose, and fulfillment in Him.

2. The Transformation of Our Desires: When we delight in the Lord, our desires are transformed. As we grow closer to God and align our hearts with His will, our desires begin to reflect His desires for us. This transformation is a work of the Holy Spirit, who shapes our hearts and minds to be more like Christ.

As our desires are transformed, we begin to desire what God desires for us. This alignment of our desires with God's will is key to experiencing the joy of fulfilled love. When our desires are in harmony with God's purposes, the fulfillment of those desires brings deep and lasting joy.

3. The Fulfillment of God's Promises: Psalm 37:4 reminds us that when we delight in the Lord, He will give us the desires of our hearts. This promise is not about God giving us everything we want; it is about God fulfilling the desires that are aligned with His will.

When love is fulfilled in this way, it is a powerful testimony to the faithfulness of God. It is a reminder that God is attentive to our desires, that He cares deeply about our happiness, and that He is faithful to fulfill His promises. This fulfillment brings not only personal joy but also a deeper understanding of God's goodness and love.

4. The Joy of Being in God's Will: The ultimate joy of fulfilled love is the joy of knowing that we are walking in God's will. In John 15:7, Jesus says, *"If you abide in me, and my words abide in you, ask whatever you wish, and it will be done for you."* This verse highlights the connection between abiding in Christ, aligning our desires with His will, and experiencing the fulfillment of those desires.

When we experience the fulfillment of love, we are reminded that we are in the center of God's will for our lives. This brings a deep sense of peace, satisfaction, and joy, knowing that we are living according to God's purposes and that His plans for us are good.

The Challenges and Rewards of Fulfilled Love

WHILE THE FULFILLMENT of love brings great joy, it also comes with its own set of challenges. These challenges are opportunities for growth, deepening our relationship with God, and strengthening our love for one another.

1. The Challenge of Maintaining the Joy: One of the challenges of fulfilled love is maintaining the joy that comes with it. It is easy to experience joy in the initial stages of fulfillment, but over time, the realities of life can sometimes dampen that joy.

To maintain the joy of fulfilled love, it is important to continue delighting in the Lord, to keep our focus on Him, and to nurture our relationship with Him and with our loved one. In Colossians 3:17, Paul writes, *"And whatever you do, in word or deed, do everything in the name of the Lord Jesus, giving thanks to God the Father through him."* This verse encourages us to keep

Christ at the center of our lives, to live with gratitude, and to find joy in all that we do.

2. The Challenge of Growing Together: Fulfilled love is not the end of the journey; it is the beginning of a new chapter. This new chapter comes with the challenge of growing together, of deepening the relationship, and of continuing to build a strong foundation of love, trust, and faith.

In Ephesians 4:2-3, Paul encourages believers to *"Be completely humble and gentle; be patient, bearing with one another in love. Make every effort to keep the unity of the Spirit through the bond of peace."* This passage reminds us that love requires effort, patience, and humility. As we grow together in love, we are called to bear with one another, to seek unity, and to work towards a deeper and more meaningful relationship.

3. The Reward of Deepened Love: The challenges of fulfilled love also bring with them the reward of deepened love. As we navigate the ups and downs of life together, our love for one another grows stronger, more resilient, and more mature.

In 1 Corinthians 13:4-7, Paul describes the characteristics of love: *"Love is patient and kind; love does not envy or boast; it is not arrogant or rude. It does not insist on its own way; it is not irritable or resentful; it does not rejoice at wrongdoing, but rejoices with the truth. Love bears all things, believes all things, hopes all things, endures all things."*

This passage highlights the depth and strength of love that is rooted in Christ. As we experience the fulfillment of love, we are invited to grow in these qualities, to deepen our love for one another, and to reflect the love of Christ in our relationship.

4. The Reward of Shared Joy: Finally, one of the greatest rewards of fulfilled love is the joy of sharing that love with others. The joy of fulfilled love is not meant to be kept to ourselves; it is meant to be shared with those around us.

In Philippians 2:2, Paul writes, *"Complete my joy by being of the same mind, having the same love, being in full accord and of one mind."* This verse reminds us that shared joy is a powerful testimony to the love of God. As we share the joy of fulfilled love with others, we spread the love of Christ and bring encouragement, hope, and joy to those around us.

Practical Steps for Embracing the Joy of Fulfilled Love

EMBRACING THE JOY OF fulfilled love requires intentionality, gratitude, and a continued focus on God's will and purposes. Here are some practical steps to help you embrace and nurture the joy of fulfilled love in your life:

1. Give Thanks to God: Begin by giving thanks to God for the fulfillment of love in your life. Gratitude is a powerful way to acknowledge God's goodness and faithfulness and to keep your focus on Him. Make it a daily practice to thank God for the love you have received and for His work in your life.

2. Keep Christ at the Center: Continue to keep Christ at the center of your relationship. Pray together, seek God's will together, and make decisions that honor Him. As you keep Christ at the center, you will find that your love for one another deepens and that your joy is sustained.

3. Nurture Your Relationship: Invest time and effort in nurturing your relationship. Communicate openly and honestly, spend quality time together, and work through challenges with patience and grace. As you nurture your relationship, you will strengthen the bond of love and create a solid foundation for the future.

4. Share Your Joy: Share the joy of fulfilled love with others. Whether it be through acts of kindness, words of encouragement, or simply by being a testimony of God's goodness, let your joy be a source of blessing to those around you. As you share your joy, you will find that it multiplies and brings even greater fulfillment.

5. Reflect on God's Faithfulness: Take time to reflect on the journey that brought you to the fulfillment of love. Remember the ways in which God has been faithful to you, even in the times of waiting and uncertainty. Let these reflections deepen your faith and strengthen your trust in God's continued work in your life.

6. Continue to Delight in the Lord: Finally, continue to delight in the Lord. Make your relationship with God your highest priority, seeking His presence, His will, and His guidance in all things. As you delight in the Lord, you will find that the joy of fulfilled love is not just a momentary experience but a lasting and life-giving reality.

Conclusion: The Joy of Love Fulfilled

THE FULFILLMENT OF love is a moment of profound joy, a time when the desires of the heart are realized and the faithfulness of God is made evident. Psalm 37:4 reminds us that this joy comes when our desires are aligned with God's will, and when we delight in Him above all else.

As you experience the joy of fulfilled love, may you be reminded of God's goodness, His faithfulness, and His deep love for you. Embrace this season of joy with gratitude, keeping Christ at the center, and sharing the blessings of love with those around you.

May the fulfillment of love in your life be a reflection of God's love for you—a love that is patient, kind, faithful, and true. And may you continue to delight in the Lord, finding your greatest joy and satisfaction in Him, as He gives you the desires of your heart.

As you journey forward, may you experience the ongoing joy of love fulfilled, knowing that it is a gift from God, a testimony to His faithfulness, and a source of blessing for you and for others. Let the joy of fulfilled love be a constant reminder of God's goodness and a celebration of His work in your life.

Chapter 15: Eternal Love as the Ultimate Fulfillment

Theological Reflection: Conclude by reflecting on the idea that earthly love is a reflection of the eternal love we have in Christ. Romans 8:38-39 can be used to discuss the unbreakable bond of God's love and how it is the ultimate love worth waiting for.

Introduction: The Longing for Ultimate Fulfillment

THROUGHOUT THE JOURNEY of life, the desire for love is a profound and driving force. Whether we seek love in the form of friendships, family bonds, or romantic relationships, the pursuit of love is central to the human experience. Earthly love brings joy, comfort, and a sense of belonging, but it also points to a deeper, more profound reality—our ultimate longing for eternal love, the love that only God can provide.

This longing for love is not merely a human desire; it is a reflection of our inherent need for connection with our Creator. Earthly love, as beautiful and fulfilling as it can be, is ultimately a reflection of the eternal love we were created for—a love that is unbreakable, unconditional, and everlasting. This eternal love is the love of God, which we experience most fully in Christ.

Romans 8:38-39 offers a powerful assurance of this eternal love: *"For I am sure that neither death nor life, nor angels nor rulers, nor things present nor things to come, nor powers, nor height nor depth, nor anything else in all creation, will be able to separate us from the love of God in Christ Jesus our

Lord."* These verses remind us that the love of God is the ultimate fulfillment of all our desires, the love that nothing in this world can ever break or diminish.

In this final chapter, we will reflect on the idea that earthly love is a reflection of the eternal love we have in Christ. We will explore the theological significance of God's eternal love, the ways in which earthly love points us to this ultimate fulfillment, and the assurance that nothing can separate us from the love of God. Drawing from Romans 8:38-39, we will conclude by considering how the unbreakable bond of God's love is the ultimate love worth waiting for and the greatest fulfillment we can ever experience.

The Theological Foundation of Eternal Love

THE CONCEPT OF ETERNAL love is foundational to Christian theology. It is rooted in the very nature of God, who is love, and is revealed through the life, death, and resurrection of Jesus Christ. This eternal love is unchanging, unconditional, and infinite—offering the ultimate fulfillment that every human heart longs for.

1. God as the Source of Eternal Love: The Bible teaches that God is the source of all true love. In 1 John 4:8, we are told that *"God is love."* This simple yet profound statement encapsulates the essence of God's nature. Love is not just something God does; it is who He is. Every act of love, every expression of kindness and grace, flows from the very character of God.

God's love is eternal, meaning it has no beginning and no end. It is not limited by time, circumstances, or human understanding. Psalm 136:1 declares, *"Give thanks to the Lord, for he is good, for his steadfast love endures forever."* This enduring love is a constant and unchanging reality, one that offers comfort and assurance in a world where so much is uncertain.

2. The Revelation of God's Love in Christ: The fullest revelation of God's eternal love is found in Jesus Christ. In John 3:16, we read, *"For God so loved the world, that he gave his only Son, that whoever believes in him should not perish but have eternal life."* This verse captures the heart of the Gospel—the good news that God's love for humanity is so great that He sent His Son to redeem us and bring us into eternal relationship with Him.

The life, death, and resurrection of Jesus are the ultimate demonstration of God's love. Through Christ, we are offered forgiveness, reconciliation, and the promise of eternal life. Romans 5:8 emphasizes this truth: *"But God shows his love for us in that while we were still sinners, Christ died for us."* This sacrificial love is the foundation of our faith and the assurance that we are loved unconditionally and eternally.

3. The Unbreakable Bond of God's Love: One of the most comforting aspects of God's love is its unbreakable nature. Romans 8:38-39 assures us that nothing can separate us from the love of God in Christ Jesus. This unbreakable bond is not dependent on our performance, our circumstances, or our worthiness. It is grounded in the character of God and the finished work of Christ.

This assurance is particularly powerful in times of doubt, fear, or uncertainty. No matter what we face in life—whether it be suffering, loss, or failure—God's love remains constant. It is a love that we can depend on, a love that provides security and hope in every season of life.

4. Eternal Love as the Fulfillment of Human Longing: Every human heart longs for love—love that is unconditional, unchanging, and everlasting. While earthly relationships can provide glimpses of this love, they are ultimately a reflection of the deeper, eternal love we were created for. C.S. Lewis, in his book *Mere Christianity,* writes about how our earthly desires point us to something greater: *"If I find in myself desires which nothing in this world can satisfy, the only logical explanation is that I was made for another world."*

This longing for eternal love is ultimately fulfilled in our relationship with God. As we come to know and experience His love, we find the satisfaction and fulfillment that our hearts have been seeking. Earthly love, while beautiful and significant, is a shadow of the perfect love that we have in Christ.

Earthly Love as a Reflection of Eternal Love

WHILE ETERNAL LOVE is the ultimate fulfillment, earthly love plays a vital role in pointing us toward this deeper reality. The love we experience in human relationships is a reflection of God's love, offering us a glimpse of the eternal and unbreakable bond we have with Him.

1. The Beauty of Earthly Love: Earthly love, in its many forms, is a gift from God. Whether it is the love between spouses, parents and children, friends, or the broader community, these relationships enrich our lives and provide us with

joy, support, and a sense of belonging. In Genesis 2:18, God declares, *"It is not good that the man should be alone; I will make him a helper fit for him."* This statement highlights the importance of relationships and the beauty of love in human life.

These relationships are a reflection of the relational nature of God. Just as God exists in a loving relationship within the Trinity—Father, Son, and Holy Spirit—so too are we created for relationship. Our ability to love and be loved is a reflection of God's image in us.

2. The Imperfection of Earthly Love: While earthly love is beautiful, it is also imperfect. Human relationships are often marked by misunderstandings, conflicts, and failures. These imperfections remind us that earthly love, while meaningful, cannot fully satisfy the deepest longings of our hearts.

The imperfections of earthly love point us to our need for God's perfect love. In 1 Corinthians 13, often referred to as the "Love Chapter," Paul describes the qualities of true love—patience, kindness, humility, selflessness. These qualities are perfectly embodied in God's love for us, but we often fall short in our human relationships. This gap between our experience of love and the ideal of love drives us to seek the fulfillment that only God's love can provide.

3. Earthly Love as a Foretaste of Eternal Love: Earthly love, though imperfect, serves as a foretaste of the eternal love we will experience in full with God. In Ephesians 5:25-27, Paul uses the analogy of marriage to describe Christ's love for the church: *"Husbands, love your wives, as Christ loved the church and gave himself up for her, that he might sanctify her, having cleansed her by the washing of water with the word, so that he might present the church to himself in splendor, without spot or wrinkle or any such thing, that she might be holy and without blemish."*

This analogy reminds us that the love we experience in marriage—or in any deep, committed relationship—is a reflection of Christ's love for us. It is a shadow of the greater reality, a glimpse of the eternal love that awaits us in our relationship with God. Just as a foretaste gives us a hint of what is to come, so too does earthly love give us a taste of the perfect, eternal love we will experience in Christ.

4. The Role of Earthly Love in Our Spiritual Growth: Earthly love also plays a significant role in our spiritual growth. Through our relationships, we

learn important lessons about love, forgiveness, patience, and grace. These lessons shape our character and help us to grow in our understanding of God's love.

In Colossians 3:12-14, Paul encourages believers to *"Put on then, as God's chosen ones, holy and beloved, compassionate hearts, kindness, humility, meekness, and patience, bearing with one another and, if one has a complaint against another, forgiving each other; as the Lord has forgiven you, so you also must forgive. And above all these put on love, which binds everything together in perfect harmony."*

This passage highlights the connection between our earthly relationships and our spiritual growth. As we practice love, forgiveness, and patience in our relationships, we grow in our likeness to Christ and deepen our understanding of His love for us. In this way, earthly love serves as both a reflection and a means of experiencing the eternal love of God.

The Assurance of God's Eternal Love

THE ASSURANCE OF GOD'S eternal love is one of the most comforting and empowering truths in the Christian faith. This love is unbreakable, unconditional, and infinite, providing us with a sense of security and hope that transcends all circumstances.

1. The Unbreakable Bond of God's Love: Romans 8:38-39 offers a powerful declaration of the unbreakable bond of God's love: *"For I am sure that neither death nor life, nor angels nor rulers, nor things present nor things to come, nor powers, nor height nor depth, nor anything else in all creation, will be able to separate us from the love of God in Christ Jesus our Lord."* This passage assures us that nothing in the universe can separate us from God's love.

This unbreakable bond is not based on our performance or our circumstances; it is based on God's character and the finished work of Christ. Because God's love is rooted in His eternal nature, it is unchanging and constant. This means that no matter what we face in life—whether it be suffering, sin, or even death—God's love remains steadfast and unshakable.

2. The Unconditional Nature of God's Love: God's love is also unconditional, meaning that it is not based on our worthiness or our ability to earn it. Ephesians 2:8-9 reminds us that *"For by grace you have been saved

through faith. And this is not your own doing; it is the gift of God, not a result of works, so that no one may boast."* This passage emphasizes that God's love and salvation are gifts of grace, not something we can earn or deserve.

This unconditional love frees us from the pressure to perform or to prove ourselves worthy of God's love. It is a love that accepts us as we are, with all our flaws and failures, and invites us into a relationship with God based on grace and mercy. This assurance allows us to live with confidence and peace, knowing that we are loved by God no matter what.

3. The Infinite Nature of God's Love: God's love is also infinite, meaning that it is without limits or end. In Psalm 103:11-12, we read, *"For as high as the heavens are above the earth, so great is his steadfast love toward those who fear him; as far as the east is from the west, so far does he remove our transgressions from us."* This passage highlights the vastness of God's love and the extent of His forgiveness.

The infinite nature of God's love means that there is no limit to His grace, mercy, and compassion. No matter how far we may stray or how great our sin may be, God's love is greater still. This infinite love offers us hope and assurance, knowing that we are never beyond the reach of God's love.

4. The Eternal Security of God's Love: Finally, God's love provides us with eternal security. In John 10:28-29, Jesus says, *"I give them eternal life, and they will never perish, and no one will snatch them out of my hand. My Father, who has given them to me, is greater than all, and no one is able to snatch them out of the Father's hand."* This passage offers a powerful promise of security in Christ.

Because God's love is eternal, it offers us security not only in this life but also in the life to come. This eternal security means that our relationship with God is not temporary or conditional; it is a permanent and unbreakable bond that will last for all eternity. This assurance allows us to live with hope and confidence, knowing that we are held in the loving hands of God forever.

Living in the Light of God's Eternal Love

AS WE REFLECT ON THE reality of God's eternal love, we are invited to live in the light of this love. This means allowing God's love to shape our identity, our relationships, and our purpose in life.

1. Finding Our Identity in God's Love: One of the most transformative aspects of God's love is the way it shapes our identity. In a world that often defines us by our achievements, our relationships, or our status, God's love offers us a different foundation for our identity.

In 1 John 3:1, we are reminded of our true identity: *"See what kind of love the Father has given to us, that we should be called children of God; and so we are."* This verse highlights the truth that our identity is not based on what we do but on who we are in Christ—beloved children of God.

When we find our identity in God's love, we are freed from the pressure to seek validation or approval from others. We no longer need to strive to prove our worth or to earn love, because we are already fully loved and accepted by God. This secure identity allows us to live with confidence, peace, and purpose.

2. Reflecting God's Love in Our Relationships: As recipients of God's eternal love, we are called to reflect that love in our relationships with others. In John 13:34-35, Jesus gives His disciples a new commandment: *"A new commandment I give to you, that you love one another: just as I have loved you, you also are to love one another. By this all people will know that you are my disciples, if you have love for one another."*

This commandment challenges us to love others as Christ has loved us—with selflessness, grace, and compassion. As we reflect God's love in our relationships, we become instruments of His love in the world, pointing others to the ultimate source of love and fulfillment.

3. Living with Purpose and Mission: God's eternal love also gives us a sense of purpose and mission in life. In Matthew 28:19-20, Jesus gives His followers the Great Commission: *"Go therefore and make disciples of all nations, baptizing them in the name of the Father and of the Son and of the Holy Spirit, teaching them to observe all that I have commanded you. And behold, I am with you always, to the end of the age."*

This commission reminds us that we are called to share the love of God with others, to make disciples, and to spread the message of the Gospel to all people. Our lives are not just about seeking our own fulfillment; they are about participating in God's mission to bring His love and salvation to the world.

4. Embracing the Hope of Eternal Life: Finally, living in the light of God's eternal love means embracing the hope of eternal life. In John 14:2-3, Jesus offers His disciples a promise: *"In my Father's house are many rooms. If it were not so, would I have told you that I go to prepare a place for you? And if I go and prepare a place for you, I will come again and will take you to myself, that where I am you may be also."*

This promise reminds us that our ultimate fulfillment is not found in this world but in the eternal life that awaits us with God. The hope of eternal life gives us perspective, helping us to live with purpose and to endure the challenges of this life with hope and faith.

Practical Steps for Embracing God's Eternal Love

EMBRACING GOD'S ETERNAL love requires intentionality, reflection, and a deepening of our relationship with Him. Here are some practical steps to help you live in the light of God's eternal love:

1. Spend Time in God's Word: Regularly spend time in Scripture, reflecting on the promises of God's love and the assurance of His eternal presence. Allow His Word to shape your understanding of His love and to strengthen your faith.

2. Cultivate a Life of Prayer: Develop a habit of prayer, bringing your needs, desires, and concerns to God. Use prayer as a way to deepen your relationship with God, to experience His love, and to seek His guidance in all areas of your life.

3. Participate in Christian Community: Surround yourself with a community of believers who can encourage you, support you, and help you grow in your faith. Engage in worship, fellowship, and service, allowing God's love to be reflected in your relationships with others.

4. Live with an Eternal Perspective: Keep your focus on the eternal hope that you have in Christ. Let this perspective guide your decisions, priorities, and relationships, helping you to live with purpose and mission.

5. Share God's Love with Others: Be intentional about sharing the love of God with those around you. Whether through acts of kindness, words of

encouragement, or sharing the Gospel, let your life be a reflection of God's love and a testimony to His goodness.

6. Rest in God's Love: Finally, take time to rest in God's love. Allow yourself to experience the peace, security, and joy that come from knowing that you are loved by God unconditionally and eternally. Let this love be the foundation of your identity and the source of your fulfillment.

Conclusion: The Ultimate Fulfillment in God's Eternal Love

AS WE CONCLUDE THIS journey, we are reminded that the ultimate fulfillment of our deepest desires is found in the eternal love of God. Romans 8:38-39 assures us that nothing can separate us from this love—a love that is unbreakable, unconditional, and infinite.

While earthly love is a beautiful and significant part of our lives, it is ultimately a reflection of the greater love we have in Christ. This eternal love is the love that we were created for, the love that satisfies the deepest longings of our hearts, and the love that offers us hope and assurance for all eternity.

As you continue on your journey, may you be encouraged to seek and embrace this eternal love. Let it be the foundation of your identity, the guide for your relationships, and the source of your hope and purpose. And as you experience the fullness of God's love, may you find the ultimate fulfillment that your heart has been longing for—a fulfillment that is found only in the unbreakable bond of God's love in Christ Jesus our Lord.

May you live in the light of this eternal love, experiencing its peace, joy, and security every day of your life. And may you be a reflection of God's love to the world, sharing the good news of His grace and mercy with all those you encounter. As you do so, may you find that this eternal love is indeed the ultimate love worth waiting for—the greatest gift and the highest fulfillment that life has to offer.

Don't miss out!

Visit the website below and you can sign up to receive emails whenever Angela Marie Stewart publishes a new book. There's no charge and no obligation.

https://books2read.com/r/B-A-LZEHC-EKHTE

About the Author

Angela Marie Stewart is a cherished author known for her heartfelt Christian romance fiction. With a passion for weaving tales that inspire faith and love, Angela's novels explore the transformative power of grace and the enduring strength of the human spirit. Her writing journey reflects her deep commitment to portraying love stories grounded in Christian values and spiritual growth. Angela's work resonates with readers seeking uplifting narratives and the comfort of faith intertwined with romance. When she's not writing, Angela enjoys community service, spending time with her family, and exploring the beauty of her surroundings.

9 798822 788474